I'M A GIGOLO

Dark, Mysterious, Malevolent

ANDREW SEGAL

To Roberta, Charlotte and Emily with thanks for their love, support and encouragement, and to Clare Newton for her enduring patience.

CONTENTS

Dear Reader   vii

Introduction   xi

1. I'm a Gigolo   1
2. The Devil's Game   11
3. The Knocking   31
4. Predators   45
5. Killing Me Softly   62
6. In his own image   72
7. Mrs Rosenfeld's Ghost   83
8. Death Zone, Everest.   104
9. Endgame   116
10. Beads of Blood   134

About the Author   147

Also by Andrew Segal   149

DEAR READER

Dear Reader,

I've been engaged in my hobby, which is writing, for about thirty years. Though I'd written a few short stories when I was a kid, at school I was written off as a literary failure. Indeed, my English teacher suggested I should totally forget authorship and try instead for a career in anything that didn't involve using my stagnant imagination.

After leaving school I started getting fresh ideas for stories, but thought no more about them until I hit on the notion of spinning a tale to my then girlfriend that I'd once been a gigolo in Cannes. She believed me, and that nearly ended the relationship, until I persuaded her, at great length, I was only joking. Today, we're still married.

Inspired by a short story by J D Salinger that left me shaken when I read the last sentence, I realised that to make a bold statement the writer has to hit the reader, with both barrels. That's when I started working on the present collection.

I hope you enjoy reading this selection of short stories as much as I've enjoyed writing them. Your comments would really be welcomed, so do let us know what you think.

Regards to you all

Andrew Segal

Tweet us @HappyLDNpress
*Instagram @**happylondonpress***
https://happylondonpress.blogspot.com
http://andrewsegalauthor.com/books/

Andrew Segal's latest novel,
The Lyme Regis Murders
Hardback, Paperback and Ebook editions are available on Amazon.
http://bit.ly/BNLymeRegisMurders

INTRODUCTION

He's gorgeous, cool and slick. Small wonder those wealthy American dames are falling over themselves to taste his flirtatious skills, just where it counts. Seduction is the name of his game, and he knows how to keep a secret. Trouble is, our Gigolo is also a mischief maker, a man with a mission - to make a killing. So he's got a secret of his own. But, can he keep it that way?

Deliciously sensual and a touch macabre, this collection of tales, I'm a Gigolo contains ten startlingly original and provocative short stories you'll need to be brave to read at bedtime.

Chapter One

I'M A GIGOLO

I am a gigolo. I like that sound. A GEEEEEEE GOH LO!!! That's right. A professional man.

My face is my fortune. My cock is my compass.

I make women happy. Not all women. Certain women. Rich women. Rich widows. Rich, American widows. At least, mostly, rich American widows.

So how do I know? Easy. 'Cos, see I'm from the old US of A. So that's how I know.

I've been in the game for maybe, ten years? It all started when I found myself unemployed and starving, bumming around in Cannes. The place was festooned with beautiful people. Girls you'd die for. Blondes, brunettes, redheads: cool, elegant, sophisticated. Legs to the sky, skin like bronzed peach on honeydew melons. Men, sleek, slick, suntanned; looking like a million dollars, (probably worth a million dollars), driving around in flash, open-top American sports cars.

That's what I wanted. But it was going to take folding stuff, long green. That's right, money. Lots of it. But how do you make a million overnight?

"Gambling," I said. But no. Wouldn't work. I was dressed like a tramp. Hell, I stank like a tramp. Still, I had to have some of it. I wanted it so bad I could practically taste the want.

My folks wanted me to be a doctor, like Dad. Or an accountant like Granddad. But all I wanted was fun.

I was good with the girls. You know what I mean. Good where it counts. Between the sheets. Nice. A considerate lover, they called me. Always let the lady come first. All the guys said I was mad. Enjoy yourself, they said. What's your problem? If she comes, she comes. You're under no obligation. She ain't paying so she ain't calling the shots. If you got what the lady wants, she'll get what she needs.

But see, that was the trouble. I didn't really have what the ladies wanted. 'Cos, like, see, I was small in that department. All the guys at school and college had like three legs. And me? Well, I had like this apology for a dong. A shrivelled worm. A cocktail sausage. A maggot's head.

But I was always careful, never let them see. Always managed to keep the little critter hidden. Had a few close escapes, but never got caught out.

Then when I started dating I made sure I made the running. Ladies seemed to like it. I never pushed, never insisted. Got to be careful. Can't get yourself accused of anything. Always let the ladies feel they had control of the situation, while it was really me that stayed in charge.

Only made the one mistake. Pretty girl. Nice type. Sympathetic. Not that I need sympathy, but you know what I mean. She was always doing things; stuff for charity, baby-sitting people's kids, helping out with old folks. She was nice. I thought I'd be okay there so I let her see the old man. Took my pants off with the light on for the first time. And guess what? She laughed. I couldn't believe it. The fucker laughed at me. Pissed herself, doubled up and wet her pants. I slunk out like a wet rat. Flat. Dead. Crushed. Beaten. A worm with a worm. Worthless piece of shit. Little dick. Small cock. Sun dried tomato.

Never again. From that day on I always kept the light out. And guess what? They never knew the difference.

They say size matters. Believe me, buster, size does not matter, at least not in the dark. Don't ask me why, but it doesn't. They just don't seem to notice. I mean if you've got like, one centimetre they'll know. But if it's just small, even if it's tiny, you're okay. As long as you can poke around inside a bit, no problem.

Swiss girl I dated said I had wonderful hands. Boy, can I work a lady with those hands. A touch, a push, a knead. Spread those thighs. Touch her little man with the fingertips. Caress it with the tongue. Feel the response. Gauge the reaction. She gasps. She squirms. She moans. She says, "Hurry, hurry, hurry", and I keep her waiting. She shouts at me, she begs, she screams, and I keep her waiting. Move away from the area, cool her down a bit, let her simmer for a while. Work on her feet, her legs. Turn her over, massage her back, move down between her buttocks. Tease her little man again, from behind. Promise her more, then let her down, for now. Roll her on her back once more and move downstairs again. Work at it and work at it. Then when she's raging, calling you every motherfucker under the sun, that's when you penetrate.

Short, sharp, quick, and hold it. Don't move. Just hold it. If you've done the groundwork the rest just follows. A long drawn out sigh. AAAAAAAAHHHHHH!!!

Success. Victory. Power. I'm a big man. As long as she doesn't see me with the light on she won't know the difference. Size matters!! The shit it does. Technique matters.

So I was good. But like I said, I was broke, and you don't make a living by being good in bed. Or do you? Lotsa rich ladies in Cannes. All over the place. Problem was, how to attract them. Sure as hell wouldn't attract them looking like I did.

So I got me a job in the kitchen of a swank hotel. Got myself cleaned up and three squares a day. Put on a bit of weight so I didn't look like something anorexic.

One of the hotel staff used to do soft furnishing repairs. Fat girl with blonde curly hair and a shy smile. Curtains needed stitching? Sofa a tiny worn patch? Call for Cilette. Rooms had to look one hundred percent all the time. Cilette said her Mum made clothes; she'd introduce me if I'd… She couldn't say it, but it was pretty obvious. So I did. It was okay too, nice and lovey dovey. Her mum was also fat, and demanding. Christ, she could go all night. End of a month I was dead. But she made me three smart suits. All in white. And three black shirts.

I started hanging out in the bars of the best hotels. Found the one I thought had the most rich-looking widows and staked my place at the bar. White suit and tie, black shirt and long black cheroot. I looked the biz.

It was easy. First one was about fifty. Sat herself down at one of the tables and ordered a margarita. She was pretty swish. Dyed strawberry blonde, expensive cream two-piece suit, dark brown accessories, shoes, handbag. Gold Rolex. She was shimmering money. I caught her eye almost at once and saw one eyebrow rise like a sort of question. Do you? Will you?

I let her stew for half an hour. Gave her an occasional glance, then went over and asked if I could buy her a drink. I'm quick with languages and I'd picked up a lot of French in my time bumming around France. So I had this brainwave; I talked to her in English, but with a French accent. If you could've seen her face. It said like, "This glamorous Frenchman is talking to little me?" So she wasn't a widow after all. She was this rich retired businesswoman. She'd built up a chain of employment bureaux and sold out for a fortune. Said she used to be a tyrant with all the staff. That told me all I needed to know about how to treat her.

Always remember, if you're going to make it in this game, you've got to understand that your performance in the sack is governed by your presentation at the start. Get that wrong and the lady holds the reins of power. You'll be treated like a nebbish and get paid peanuts. Get it right and you earn the lady's respect and up goes the price she'll pay.

So what are the golden rules, I hear you ask? Easy. And they're all as old as time. You always treat a lady like a hooker and a hooker like a lady. I know, I know, you've heard it before. But let me tell you why. It confuses them and at the same time it impresses them. It says you're different from the rest, and that makes them interested. And you've got to keep them interested if you're going to milk it for all you can. Be gentle, be kind, be considerate of them and be curious about their backgrounds. Let them do most of the talking. Listen attentively, then lose your temper, over some triviality. Blow up. Explode. Reduce them to tears, then pacify 'em, win them round with a reassuring smile and a paternal pat on the shoulder.

In short, keep 'em guessing. Never let 'em know where they stand. You'll have the bitches eating out of the palm of your hand. And the sex'll be terrific.

Next thing. Know your food and wines. Be assured in hotels and restaurants, particularly when ordering. It demonstrates your power and control over people. Very aphrodisiac. Be confident in shops, particularly when it comes to them buying you gifts. Settle for nothing less than the best. Never sell yourself short. They didn't, your clients, and that's why they're where they are today. That's how you'll get where they are.

Be funny. They like that: a sense of humour. Put on the little lost boy act, appear vulnerable; they'll think they can mother you. Then just as they imagine they're back in control, holding the reins again, have a tantrum, blow your top, sulk. Then forgive them and take them to bed. It never fails.

Finally, and this is important, they're all into astrology. Learn your star signs, mug up on a bit of palmistry and they'll believe you're the bloody prophet Elijah.

So what did I do with the strawberry blonde? I'll tell you what I did. I was everything I said you should be, but in between all the gentlemanly behaviour, I treated her like shit. She'd never had anyone dare before, they'd all cow-towed to her. This was something new. The more I raged, the more she came on like a lamb. Bought me diamond studded gold cufflinks, clothes, leather goods and gave me an allowance. In return, I fucked her rigid. I was the first one who didn't give a toss for her, 'cos she wasn't employing me. And boy, did she love it. Said she felt like a kid again. I was in charge, and Christ it felt good. I kept threatening to end the relationship. The more I said I'd go, the more she used to come. Told me I was the best lover she'd ever had. I always remembered to keep the light off, let her think it was more romantic that way. And I always kept up the French accent. That part was no problem, by now my French was so good I was easy about using the language all the time.

On nights off, times when she'd see her own friends when there wasn't a place for me, I'd grab the old white suit and tie, black shirt and cheroot and soak up a few dry ones, shaken not stirred, at my favourite hotel bar. I attracted them like flies. Thing is, money attracts money, and with my allowance I was feeling pretty good about myself and it showed. I could afford to pick and choose. They came to me like lambs to the slaughter.

About this time I was starting to get bored with the strawberry blonde. The sex was getting samey and her tits had sagged too much. I felt I was worth more than the allowance she was doling out, but she disagreed. So I left her. I let her down gently. Did it the professional way, no point in creating unnecessary conflict. Said the whole thing was too much for me, that she'd grown and developed, moved on, that we both needed to spread our wings, fly higher into the sun. All that sort of crap. Of course she cried, and I consoled her, let her know I'd always be there for her spiritually. Then I pissed off.

After that there was a whole raft of women, each one richer than the last. Picking them out was getting easier; I could smell the cash, sense the prosperity, inhale the essence of luxury. Yum!

The gifts were getting more generous, the allowances were getting bigger and I was getting richer. Nice feeling. I realised how much I'd been selling myself short with that first one. It wouldn't happen again.

I still kept up the accent and I still kept the light out. After all, a professional man has his reputation to maintain. Lots of them thought I had a dong the size of the Sears Roebuck Tower. All psychological, see? All in the build up like I said.

Thankfully, I never had trouble getting a hard on. There may not have been much to play with, but what there was needed to be hard enough to penetrate. Thing is, I was getting bored with servicing a lot of old bags just for the loot. I'd been careful about the money, invested it, saved it and so on, and I was comfortable. Not rich, but pretty okay. Still, a professional man doesn't stop working just because he's got a decent stash. I could afford to enjoy what I did, be a bit more choosy. So I had a few affairs just for the hell of it, not business, just fun. I kept thinking about some of those bastards who'd laughed at me when I was at school, felt it was time for a bit of payback.

Then I met this girl whose husband was some big time doctor. When she told me his name, I nearly flipped. Daniel Lisle had been the prize piss-taker in the days when I'd had to endure the college communal shower. While he was around I got labelled, `The Dwarf'. The Dwarf!! Can you believe it? He was due to meet his little lady a week after her arrival in Cannes, some conference back home having held him up. So, like, I fucked her till neither of us could stand up. The more I fucked, the better I felt. This one's for you, Lisle, you sonofabitch, and this, and this.

The buzz was indescribable and I decided I wanted more of it. So I started screwing every married woman I could find, every `young', married woman I could find. Each time I'd imagine her husband's face if he knew, as long as he didn't know my little secret. I was having a ball, balling the world. Payback time, you fucking scum. And who's laughing now?

Then I had this great idea. And what a great idea it was. Like killing two birds with one stone. It was so simple. I'd get a cock job. Know what I mean? You got it, a penis extension, one of the latest ops. And who would I get to do it? You guessed again, Doctor Daniel Lisle. The very same. Then I'd fuck his wife some more, before persuading her to make a tearful admission to her husband. He was rich, really rich. They'd divorce, she'd collect half, and we'd both ride off into the sunset. WHOOOPPEEE!!

So I arranged an appointment with the eminent doctor. Of course I'd changed a bit since he last saw me; still I decided to take no chances. I'd grown this pencil moustache, very French. And I wore a pair of flash Cartier shades. I spoke to him in the old French accent and the pisser didn't notice a thing. He said the op' would cost me a packet and that he could arrange for it to be carried out at a local private hospital. After I'd got over the surgery I reckoned I'd go on a spree. Fuck every married woman from Cannes to Calais. With the lights on. My mouth watered at the prospect. Then come back and help myself to his wife.

So I present myself at the clinic. The place is five star. I mean nothing but the best. Gold plated showers, silk sheets and carpet pile you could get lost in. Guys, I tell you, if you realised the luxury you could live in while some gullible schmuck gives you a bigger cock to screw his wife with, you'd all be coughing up the dough.

I mean, don't think I wasn't nervous. Let's face it, when a guy puts his manhood under the knife, that's got to be a cause of concern. You gotta just keep thinking of the ladies and what you're going to be doing for them. You'll all be God's gift. Or maybe, Doctor Lisle's gift.

After the op' I wake up and I'm feeling kinda groggy. A bit sore down there, like someone stuck something in it. But I don't want to look down, not just yet. I'll wait for the good doctor.

After a while he comes in. Doctor Lisle. White coat. Tall guy, dark hair, neat cut. Looking rich. Looking confident. Year round tan. Like the sun shines outta his ass. The mug still doesn't know. And he starts talking to me like an old friend. Says life ain't so great for him right now. As if I care. But I let the sucker go on.

Tells me his wife's having an affair. *Ho! Ho! Ho!* I think. I wonder who with. I try to look sympathetic, but I'm bustin' to laugh. Seems she confided in him. Oh! Wow! I think. Funny thing is, she tells him, the guy had a tiny cock. Odd, I could've sworn I left the light out. Fact, I know I left the light out. So how'd she know?

Doctor gives me a funny look. "Isn't that your problem, sir?" he enquires politely.

"Not any more," I grin. "You fixed that all for me, doc," I say. And I'm thinking, what the hell else does he think I'm doing here? He's the surgeon who's changed it all for me. So I say, "How's the old pecker, doc? What've you given me, eight inches? Ten?" And I'm practically crying, the whole thing's so funny.

Then the doc gives me this sort of grave look and says, "Ah!"

So I say, "What's, Ah, doc?"

And he says, "Well we gave you a routine once over

before we operated. The usual precaution you know." And he's kinda talking like he thinks there's something funny, and I tell him to get on with it. So he goes on, "We discovered you had an enlarged prostate and decided to correct that problem before we concentrated on the penile enlargement operation which will now have to be carried out at a future date."

Now I'm puzzled, so I lift the sheets and see what looks like a bottle of piss hanging off the side of the bed being slowly filled from a transparent tube sticking out of the end of my dick. My little untouched, unchanged dick. Right now I'm not feeling so good, so I ask the doc when I can come in for the enlargement and he says in about three to four months, and that makes me feel better again. But like, see, the doc still acts like something's very funny. He's got this little smile, like a mouse having its balls squeezed, playing at the corners of his mouth.

Then I ask him about the prostrate, or whatever it's called, and he says everything is just fine and I'll have no more trouble passing urine in the future.

"Great," I say. "'Cept I didn't know I was having trouble in the first place. Anything else?" I ask.

"Yes." He smiles. "I'm afraid that from now on you'll be totally impotent. Bit like one of Snow White's little friends, I'm afraid." And the fucker's got this fat grin on his face as he says it. "Now, when did you want to come in for that second operation?"

I book the date for three months' time. And I can't wait. So what if I can't get it up? Who gives a shit? With my hands... Listen, women are all mugs. They'll never know the difference.

Chapter Two

THE DEVIL'S GAME

"Faites vos juex." The croupier was in her late twenties, in six inch heels, with an absurdly short, black flared skirt, revealing white, thigh high stockings and occasional glimpses of white cutaway knickers. Her black, sleeveless waistcoat was designed to reveal an ample décolletage and whenever she moved her head her long blond ponytail swung around tantalisingly.

The several, mainly young men at the table were all seemingly transfixed by her, unable to decide whether to concentrate on her legs, breasts or tiny briefs. All, that is, except one man; in his early forties, with neat cut, black hair, a slim moustache and pointed beard, elegantly turned out in a white dinner jacket with red bow tie and matching pocket handkerchief. He'd seen it all before, and if he was aware of the croupier's striking looks, he revealed no interest, merely concentrating on the mounting pile of chips in front of him.

He looked bored, or otherwise engrossed, and, ignoring the house rules, chain smoked black, clove cigarettes. Known as kreteks, which, contrary to popular misconception, weren't guaranteed to enhance health or prolong life, comprising some 80% tobacco and 20% ground cloves, cinnamon and other herbs.

His eyes were shadowed, it was almost 3.00am and he'd been at the blackjack and backgammon tables for several hours before bringing his accumulated winnings to the roulette table for a last splash prior to turning in. He'd done well this night. Gambling was more than a profession, it was a lifestyle, a means of pitting yourself against the odds. He'd been having strange dreams recently; predictive whisperings in his head in the dead of night. Worth a try? He was a gambler. But he wouldn't, at least not this time.

"Monsieur?" The croupier looked in the direction of the man enquiringly. He pondered for a moment, then pushed the whole pile of chips on to black. The croupier raised an eyebrow, but spun the wheel her blond ponytail swinging with the movement. Several pairs of eyes at the table were transfixed, young men leaning forward to get a clearer view as the roulette ball leapt around and around, before hovering uncertainly and then finally settling on number 27, red.

There was a sigh of apparent sympathy for the gambler, with an unspoken sense that he would now walk away. A loss of that apparent size would be enough for most gamblers in one session. But instead the man wrote something on a notepad he'd taken from an inside pocket and, tearing out the page, handed it to the croupier.

She looked perplexed for a moment, then said, "Monsieur wishes me to take his IOU and to double his stake?"

"That's right," said the man, extracting a gold Dunhill and lighting another cigarette. He inhaled, deeply, then, leaning back, blew a jet of smoke towards the ceiling. A buzz went round the table, and some gamblers from other parts of the casino began to congregate around the man, with inquisitive looks.

The croupier caught the eye of one of the watchers, a white haired man in his sixties, wearing a black dinner jacket and purple velvet bow-tie. He nodded, almost imperceptibly, and the IOU was accepted.

The gambler indicated, black, once more, and the IOU was

duly laid on the black square. More people clustered around, and the croupier again spun the wheel. The little white ball jumped around like an excited puppy. People strained forward as the ball bounced into a red pocket, then a black, finally settling in a red. This time there was a gasp from those assembled.

The gambler felt the merest flutter in the pit of his stomach, before writing out another note for the croupier. "Monsieur wishes to double his stake? Yet again?"

The gambler drew on his cigarette. Squinted as smoke drifted into his eyes, and stopped for a moment as he thought he caught sight of a man in a white coat in the mirror facing the table he was at. The man was staring at him intently. The gambler spun round to confront the watcher, but despite looking among the crowd, could find no-one. Shrugging inwardly, he turned back to the croupier. "That's right." He said, "Black again." He closed his eyes for a moment. Weighed the odds, if one could. Hard to judge with a game as random as roulette. He could hear conversation all around him, but it was a mere hum in the back of his head. Hardly a distraction.

The white haired man took slightly longer before nodding to the croupier, who put the IOU on the black, then spun the wheel. She looked nervous and nearly fumbled the ball as she flicked it into the bowl.

At the same moment as she let go the ball, when all bets had been placed, the gambler, remembering the dreams, suddenly reached forward, transferring the IOU from the black square to the red. This time, he thought, I will. Not all casinos will take bets once the ball is in the bowl, but this one did.

Again there was a murmur from those crowding around as the ball ricocheted from place to place, before seeming to settle in a black slot, bringing forth muttered comments of, 'Shame.' But as its momentum died, the ball bounded one final time, and, against expectation, settled in a red slot.

The gambler found himself being clapped on the back, and

surrounded by congratulating gamblers. Without a comment, he rose, and, catching the white haired man's attention said, "Three percent for the staff. I'll take a cheque, to cash please." He stalked off to the cashier. The atmosphere around him was hot and sticky. He flapped away cigarette smoke from his eyes. Despite the calm demeanor, his pulse was racing. Close call tonight, he thought. Odd dreams. Then smiled to himself.

Outside the casino the man wandered towards the sound of the sea, his patent leather shoes crunching the gravel in the drive. The gentle whoosh of the waves and smell of salt in the air had a soothing effect, settling his mood. It had been a long night. He'd contravened his own rules and been reckless, but he'd won. Those nighttime fanatsies? He wouldn't be inclined to take that sort of chance again. But he *was* a gambler. That wouldn't change.

The palm trees moved gently in the early morning breeze, their shadows swaying over the front lawns of his hotel nearby. A humid night, sultry. Peaceful. Once again, he thought he saw the image of a white coated man up ahead of him, walking quickly away; but the gambler shook his head. Hallucinations, he thought. Need to sleep. Neck and back muscles ache.

She'd be waiting for him in their suite.

He stopped to turn back, and stubbed out the cigarette butt in the hotel entranceway, suddenly, almost doubling up with pain as a needle point of agony speared his gut taking is breath away.

He stood still until the spasm passed, then with sweat running down his face and neck, made his way in.

The lights were out, and he moved as silently as he could, closing the door with the smallest of clicks; but she must have heard him, or was perhaps waiting for his return.

He heard her shuffle the sheets and sit up in the dark. "Bryce?" she whispered.

"It's me, Jenna."

She was a strawberry blond, Scandinavian model, with high

cheek bones and almond eyes. "God, darling. What time is it? I tried to stay up, but was just so tired." She spoke unaccented English, having spent part of her teens in an English finishing school in Switzerland.

"It's 3.30am. Go back to sleep. I'm taking a shower, then I'll be with you."

"Mmmmm! Missed you."

"Missed you too."

"How did it go? Did you win?"

"Yes darling, I came first."

"Silly boy," she giggled, and snuggled under the sheets. "What did you play tonight? Blackjack? Poker?"

"No, for a change I played, the Devil's Game."

"The Devil's Game?" she murmured.

"Roulette."

"Oh! And why's it the Devil's Game?"

"Because, darling, when you add up all the numbers on a roulette wheel, they total 666."

But she was already asleep. He lay next to her feeling the gentle rise and fall of her breathing; this woman he loved. Leaning on one elbow, he looked over at Jenna's sleeping form, at her golden hair, fanned over the pillow and felt a pang of guilt, knew he was neglecting her, spending too much time at the tables. If anything happened to him…. He'd have to go to that clinic in New York and get himself checked out. Something clearly very wrong. Probably an ulcer. New York Presbyterian Hospital, ranked number one in the US, as soon as he could get a flight.

Bryce had a restless night, what there was left of it. He worried constantly about his heavily autistic son, being cared for at one of America's finest centres in Atlanta, Georgia. Bryce's first wife, Hillary, had died as a result of complications during and after the birth. Bryce had hired UK nannies when he realised he would not be able to cope alone. Once he'd discovered that

Jason was autistic he'd arranged for care at the professional centre the boy was at, at present.

Fate, never content to deliver one blow at a time, had dealt a second one. The boy had been born with a hole in the heart, and being premature and small, an operation had been delayed and delayed. Bryce saw the boy, accompanied by Jenna, his long term girlfriend, as regularly as he could. The treatment centre was a cost to be born; the heart operation would be a considerable added expense. He couldn't afford to take any more arrogant risks at the gaming tables. He needed cash, a great deal of it.

He was in a deep sleep when he heard the voice. "Bryce," it whispered.

Bryce shivered, icy cold fingers running down his back. The dream again? "Who is that?"

"A friend," the voice responded.

"What do you want?"

"To help you. I'm here to help you."

"Oh, and how are you going to do that?"

"You need money. A lot of it."

Bryce turned onto his side. The voice went on, "I can help you get it; if you will trust me."

"Who are you, and why should you help me? Why should I trust you?"

"Because you have no choice. And anyway, let's say I like to play little games. They amuse me. You might say I'm a bit of a gambler; just like you. After all, I guided you just now. You had a big win."

Bryce turned restlessly again, "Let me sleep."

"I will. I will. Just listen to me, and I'll prove to you that I can help again." The whispering went on.

"Get on with it, then," said Bryce, impatiently.

"Tomorrow night; well tonight, actually, I want you to go to a casino on the other side of the island. Nassau has lots to choose from. This one is called The Gold Ingot. They won't know you there, and there won't be the embarrassment of possible disbarment after a win like the one you've just had."

"Then what?"

"Then you'll put 20,000 dollars on black 26, and wait to see what happens. Place the bet as close to midnight as you can. It's important."

"Are you mad? I'd never bet like that from cold. 20,000 dollars?"

"Bryce, you won more than twice that just now. What have you got to lose, if you'll pardon the pun? If you win you'll be a long way towards those two lots of medical fees you need to fund. Try me. You don't know how misunderstood I am."

"What do you mean, two lots of medical fees? And, misunderstood? How, misunderstood?"

But the voice had disappeared. There was just a black silence.

The white light hurt his eyes. His tongue was swollen, his mouth, gummy and his scalp itched. Then he remembered, he'd won again last night. He pretty well always won. Could that alter? The gamblers' mantra: if you're losing, keep playing till your luck changes. If you're winning, carry on with that winning streak. Either way, don't lose your nerve.

So when *did* you stop? Only when you'd nothing left to gamble with? Or nothing left to gamble for. What place was Bryce in right now? He needed a lot of money, and soon. He gambled his way though life, putting little aside for contingencies. Medical expenses loomed. 26 black, the voice had said. That dream.

Bryce was neither superstitious nor religious; although he'd thought about praying for his son on one or two occasions. Trouble was, he didn't know how to pray, or who to pray to. He'd tried to pray for his wife. There'd been no response. Just hollow silence. 26 black. Whose voice was that?

He could hear Jenna in the shower. She was humming. She was happy. She came out, still shiny wet, wrapping a bath sheet around her. Then she caught his eye, and let the towel drop.

Long legs, firm breasts, flat tummy. Every time he saw her like this, it was like the first time. Always took his breath away.

"Big boy's awake," she grinned, quickly climbing in beside him. She smelled of Camay and Chanel No 5.

"Darling, I need to shower again and brush my teeth."

"Fuck your teeth," she whispered, cuddling up to him.

"I'd rather fuck you," he said.

"God, you talk a lot, don't you," she whispered, wrapping herself around him.

They had coffee, and hot croissants dripping with butter, delivered by room service, and sat, in towelling robes, enjoying the late breakfast. He'd told her about the dream. "It's not the way I play," he'd said.

She steepled her hands and rested her forehead against them. "I know. But this is not your bet, is it? You needn't worry your judgement's failing, because this crazy dream isn't you. It's something else.

To get through the day, they went deep sea fishing, Bryce and Jenna. He caught two large Blue Marlin. Got back to the hotel, exhausted, but unwound.

"What's it to be Bryce?" she enquired. She'd flopped into one of the armchairs, still in her bikini and sarong, and lay back with her sun-bronzed legs stretched out.

"What do *you* think?"

"You've never asked me that sort of thing before. Bryce, it isn't my world, it's yours. What do you want me to say?"

He stood gazing out the window. The sea was calm and the sun was going down fast, shadows lengthening into a magnificent Caribbean sunset. "It doesn't make sense, Jenna. Alright, it was a vivid dream. But that's all it was, nothing more."

"Darling, you asked me, so I'll tell you what I think. Why not go for it? What have you got to lose? You won enough last night to be able to take the chance. You'll never know unless you try."

"You offering me the apple, Eve?"

"I'm offering you the apple. Knowledge is king, and you need to know. You want to know."

"Come with me?"

She smiled, "I'll come with you."

They wandered around the casino for what seemed to him like hours, but was in fact just thirty minutes. He dabbled at Blackjack, and then at Baccarat before wandering over to the Roulette table. He felt restless, out of his comfort zone. The casino was musty, smoky; had an unfamiliar feel to it. He couldn't just put 20,000 dollars on a specified number, it would invite, comment? Suspicion? He made a number of desultory forays, winning a few, losing a few. Initially betting a few hundred dollars at a time, then gradually upping the ante to two, three and four thousand dollar stakes.

Jenna stood behind him, her hands on his shoulders. She was dressed soberly in a navy blue, knee length, sleeveless, halterneck, her locks held back with a diamante hair clip. Bryce was beginning to attract attention, with the size of his bets, although his pot was little changed from when he'd first come in. He thought he'd seen the man in the white coat again, but demurred from asking Jenna if she'd seen anything.

He was also beginning to feel nervous. An almost unique experience, his pulse gently thudding in his chest, his palms sweating. Jenna, sensing it, leaned over him and whispered in his ear, "Now Bryce; go for it. It's coming up to midnight. You need to know. Now or never."

Bu he hesitated. "Not sure I can."

It was the first time Jenna had ever heard him sound uncertain about anything.

"Come on!" she urged, impatiently. "Don't let me down now."

He breathed in deeply; paused a moment longer, then said, "Okay, I'll go for black. I can't go for the number 26 as well. It's asking too much."

"Faites vos jeux," announced the croupier.

"Your call," said Jenna. "I'm backing you. Whatever."

Bryce frowned, thought, 'I can't keep doing this,' and pushed 20,000 dollars-worth of chips onto the black, then sat back as the croupier spun the wheel and flicked the white ball in the opposite direction into the bowl. Bryce adjusted his bow tie, loosened it, then tightened it, heard the murmur from the others around the table at the size of the bet. Felt Jenna's grip on his shoulders. In the silence that followed the ball as it juddered around the bowl, Bryce felt suspended, floating, out of body and out of control.

Moments later, the ball landed in the black 26 pocket. There was a gasp from those around the table, and a ripple of applause.

"That's it," said Bryce, throwing some chips towards the croupier. "I'm done."

Back at the hotel Jenna flung her arms around Bryce's neck, pressed herself up against him, "You did it, darling."

Bryce sounded contemplative, "That's right, I did. Not some night-time hallucination. Just my own intuition." He sounded surprised. He felt surprised, relieved. But also, confirmed in his own mind, that he was a winner. Gambling within his own bounds he'd always be a winner. This night's outrageous bet, the second of its size, was not to be repeated. As a professional gambler one took calculated risks, kept winnings modest, but constant. Bryce could have chalked up a fortune, if he'd wished, but he'd have probably found himself banned from many casinos.

Of course there were those who bet in hundreds of thousands, sometimes winning millions.

Arab oil billionaires, businessmen like the Australian, Kerry Packer, who won and also lost, millions. But they were known, and accepted by the casinos who took the good times with the bad. Usually, that is, but not always.

In 2004, Philip Green, the billionaire owner of the Arcadia group of companies, won £2 million in a single session at the Les

Ambassadeur's Club in London's Mayfair. He went on to win a further £1 million in following sessions, months later. The club issued a profits warning and came close to insolvency.

All those wealthy gamblers played as a pastime. They had other sources of income and weren't rich just from gambling.

"What's next Bryce?" Jenna had slipped into a white, ankle length, diaphanous negligee, which emphasised the tanned body beneath.

But Bryce was distracted. "Sleep, darling. I need to think, and I do that best when semi-unconscious. It's been a long day."

Bryce could stay alert when playing for 24 hours and more, but right now, it wasn't necessary and he was asleep in moments.

Then he heard the voice again, intruding on his thoughts, "Hello Bryce."

Bryce twisted and turned agitatedly as he slumbered, marbled veins of fear running through him. "Who the hell is that? Who's there?"

"It's me Bryce, your friend."

"You're not my friend. What do you want?"

"You didn't take my advice, mon ami."

"I didn't need to. I'm a professional gambler. I went with my gut."

"No you didn't; you chickened out on my tip. If you'd listened to me, and done as I recommended, you'd have won enough to cover all those medical expenses."

"Go away. Let me sleep."

But the voice clung to him like a limpet. "Not yet. You know, I'm a gambler, too. But you need to believe I know what I'm talking about. So I'm going to prove to you that I can do all I promise."

"Really?"

"I'm going to say this just once, so listen carefully. Tomorrow night at The Gold Ingot, the same casino as tonight, at exactly 11.43 pm you will place a bet of 50,000 dollars on red 34."

"Ridiculous," said Bryce on his sleep.

"At odds of 35 to 1, you'll walk away with, 1.75 million dollars. Enough to cover all those medical expenses. You'll be banned from the club. But that will hardly matter, will it?"

"Who are you?"

"I told you, a friend."

"The Angel Gabriel?"

"Hardly."

"Well who then?"

"Who do you think?"

"Well, you're not God; that's for sure."

"Doesn't leave much does it?"

"Old Nick, then?"

"Proud to make your acquaintance."

"I'm going to sleep."

"Red 34. 11.43 pm. Don't forget. Don't let me down."

Light was flooding the room. Jenna rubbed her eyes and sat up in bed. "You were restless in the night, darling. I heard you talking in your sleep; as if you were having a conversation with someone."

Bryce turned on his side, propped his head on an upturned palm and looked up at Jenna, "I had that dream again; this time it's insisting I bet on red 34, and at precisely 11.43 pm. But it said I should bet; wait for it; 50,000 dollars this time."

Jenna pondered, then said, softly, "Wow! That is quite a sum. It's not even as if roulette is your game. Isn't yours blackjack?"

"That, or poker, if the stakes are right."

"Bryce; honestly, what are the odds on your winning? Has anyone ever really won big?"

"Only ever a handful, but of truly spectacular wins. In 1873, over a number of days, one Joseph Jagger, rumoured to be related to Mick Jagger, won 325,000 dollars at the casino in Monte Carlo. A stupendous sum, by any standards. He invested it in property in Yorkshire, and died, a rich man."

"And that's it?"

"No, in 1891 Charlie Wells, a small time conman, using the so called Martingale technique, which I used the other night, where you double your bets whenever you lose, broke the bank at Monte Carlo. A million francs in one night, a feat he repeated later that same year. No-one was entirely sure how he did it, but he walked away with a fortune, which he subsequently lost, later serving eight years in jail for fraud, and finally dying penniless in 1926. Charlie's middle name was, Deville."

"God, that is so weird," Jenna murmured.

"There've also been more recent big winners, as well as Phil Green, there's Mike Ashley, a billionaire businessman, who won £1.3 million on a single spin of the wheel, and left the casino after just 15 minutes, saying 'That'll do me, thanks very much.' And others. There's always some. But big winners don't always get allowed back to the clubs they've taken money from."

"Will they let you back into The Gold Ingot?"

"Probably, this once. They'll be hoping to win back what I've just walked away with."

"And if you bet 50,000 dollars, what do you stand to win?"

"Darling, if I won, and that's a big, 'IF,' I'd walk away with 1.75 million dollars. They'd never let me back in there again. I doubt they'd even let me drive past the place."

"What are you going to do?"

"I'm going to go fishing again. Coming?"

"Sure. Let's eat first though."

He caught nothing, and didn't feel relaxed at the end of a frustrating day at sea.

They arrived at the casino at around 10.00pm. Bryce felt edgy, and smoked one cigarette after another. As before, he played at some of the other tables; winning here, losing there. At 10.30pm he sat down at the roulette table, with Jenna standing behind him. She was in a black, backless evening gown which contrasted strikingly with the strawberry blond mane that tumbled over her shoulders.

The croupier was a stick thin, dinner jacketed young man

with black hair down the back of his neck. Despite the somewhat muted lighting, he affected dark glasses.

One or two people at the table recognized Bryce, but he made no show of remembering them.

Bryce bet carefully. The spin of the wheel produces such random results it wasn't difficult to maintain a fairly even balance between his winning and losing plays. Over the course of an hour, with nothing to show beyond a gradual increasing of his stake, which itself attracted some comment, the attention he'd garnered the other night had barely materialised this time. The one thing that did draw some attention was the pile if chips he'd sat down with. 60,000 dollars. A mountain of plastic money.

At 11.30, Bryce was 2,000 dollars down. He had 58,000 dollars in front of him. He'd been betting consistently on a colour, with even odds it wasn't too hard to keep wins and losses within bounds.

Now he made his first targeted play. He put 1,000 dollars on red 3. There was a muttering of comment around the table. Black 24 came up.

Bryce then doubled his stake to 2,000 dollars, picking black 11. The croupier spun the wheel and the ball bounced around before settling in black 17.

He now had 55,000 left in front of him. It was 11.35pm. Eight minutes to go. Bryce lit up another cigarette and tried to look disinterested. But he could feel his shirt beginning to stick to his back. The atmosphere in the casino was becoming oppressive. He pushed 5,000 dollars onto black 17. The table hushed. The wheel spun and the ball landed in red 34, the pocket right next to black 17. There were cries of, 'Quelle dommage,' and, 'Bad luck old boy.'

Jenna leaned over Bryce's shoulder and whispered. "You okay?"

"Not sure," he whispered back.

The croupier was calling, "Faites vos jeux."

Players placed chips all over the baize. There was a bustle of activity.

Jenna leaned over his shoulder again, displaying an expanse of décolletage. "Yes?"

Bryce paused.

"Knowledge darling" she urged. "We need to know. Tree of knowledge, and all that."

Bryce pondered, "Hmmm! I know; but wasn't that followed by the exit from Eden? We'll see."

The croupier was preparing to close off the bets. Bryce glanced at his watch. It was 11.43pm. Then he noticed another player at the table, one he'd not been aware of till now; an elderly, grey faced, man in a white coat. Bryce suddenly felt a stab of pain like the one he'd experienced the other night. He winced as steel pliers cut into his intestines.

Too late? The croupier announced, "Rien ne va plus," at the same time as Bryce pushed his whole pot of 50,000 dollars onto red 34. There was a gasp around the table, and a crowd of onlookers quickly materialised, shouldering each other in an attempt to get a better view. The croupier looked up and over Bryce's shoulder. Jenna saw him nod to someone out of her field of vision, and thought she saw the shadow of a smile on the young man's face. The casino would make back all Bryce had won the other night, and more.

It was then that Jenna had second thoughts; realised her mistake; she shouldn't have pushed so hard. Too late. A bleak time beckoned.

Bryce lit another cigarette and blew smoke towards the ceiling. Looking around, he found yet again that the white coated man was not to be seen. Just exhausted, he thought. Imagining things. But he wasn't nervous any more. The bet was laid and he was ice cold calm, the way he liked to be. He placed his hands on the table in front of him, his cigarette in the right. He smiled at the croupier, and nodded at some of the other players who looked back at him, fascinated. He wouldn't win, but he was resigned to losing. Impossible odds. Accept your fate when you've no choice.

"Rien ne vas plus," repeated the croupier, and spun the wheel. A moment later he flicked the ball into the bowl in the opposite direction to the wheel. It bounced around crazily.

Bryce hardly looked. It was as if the bet was of no importance to him whatsoever. He drew again on the cigarette, a hum of activity around him as though from another place. People strained forward.

Jenna was now regretting even more that she'd encouraged the bet. It was a mistake. She had faith in Bryce, but she'd been the one to push it. She straightened up and held her breath.

The ball bounced around erratically, into and out of several pockets, before looking to settle in black 4, to a hushed and disbelieving, "Nooooo," from the crowd, much as the other night. He'd lost. All over. Then just as before, with the last of its momentum the little ball jumped one final hop landing in red 34.

For a moment there was not a sound. Then the casino erupted with cries of congratulation, accompanied by people slapping Bryce on the back, kissing Jenna and seemingly wanting to hug them both.

Bryce got up from the table, gathering his winnings; 1.75 million dollars, before tossing a handful of chips to the croupier, who nodded acknowledgement. Bryce looked as though this was an everyday occurrence, and felt oddly detached from everything and everyone. At the cashier's desk he handed over details of a Swiss bank account and gave instructions for an immediate transfer of funds. The operation took no more than fifteen minutes, and Bryce had the bank confirm receipt to him.

Nodding at Jenna, Bryce said, "Time to go," and she linked her arm through his, leaned against him. The crowd, applauding politely, made way for Bryce and Jenna as they sauntered towards the exit. At the exit, a large, dinner jacketed man with a vast paunch and oily, ginger hair, leaned over to talk to Bryce.

His breath smelled of whisky. "You will not be welcome here again, Monsieur. Or anywhere else on the island. You understand me?"

Bryce nodded, but said nothing.

Overlooking 5th Avenue and Central Park South, The Plaza Hotel, designated, a National Historic Monument, was the last word in old world elegance and luxury. Bryce had flown to New York for medical tests as soon as he could after the big wins in Nassau. He'd also set in motion examinations for his boy, who was now old enough and strong enough to undergo hole in the heart surgery.

Bryce had been subjected to a battery of tests over a number of days, and was now awaiting results. He was drained and suffering increasing pain. "Tomorrow," he said to Jenna. I really need to know."

"It's getting worse?"

"Much."

She lay down next to him, under the duvet, "Try to get some rest, darling."

He'd taken a powerful sleeping draught, nothing would disturb him.

Bryce slumbered peacefully, Jenna cuddled up next to him. All was quiet. Then he heard it again. The echo of a sound. The voice. "Well done, Monsieur. You took my advice. Red 34."

"You!"

"Yes, me."

"What do you want?"

"You might want to thank me."

"For what?"

"Oh come, my friend. 1.75 million dollars, for a start." The voice sounded testy.

Bryce turned on to his back. He felt fully awake now. "This is a dream. It's my gut feeling, that's all. I placed a long odds bet and won. I am a winner."

"I know one thing, mon ami."

"What's that." Bryce stared upwards. He was having a conversation with himself.

"You are one arrogant bastard."

"Bryce. You're talking to yourself." She was barely awake.

"Go to sleep Jenna," he muttered. "I'm a bit restless."

He stared on at the ceiling.

The voice said, "Tell me, do you ever lose?"

Bryce paused, thought about it, "Actually no, I don't. Well, seldom." Bryce wasn't sure he believed his own boast. Of course he lost at times, but now wasn't the time to admit it. His intuition warned him that to show weakness would be dangerous, possibly fatal. The voice was more than just a dream.

The voice came back, sounding more irritated than before. "As a man who never loses, would you be prepared to bet on anything?"

"I said I seldom lose, not never. Anyway, it depends on the odds."

"Consider this," the voice said. "Is there anything at all that you would actually stake your life on?"

"Only one thing."

"Well?"

"That we all die one day."

"Interesting," said the voice. "Because I know something you don't, about your health."

"Really?"

"Yes, and it's not good news."

"Tell me?"

"Those stomach pains you've been experiencing."

"What do you know about my stomach pains?"

"You forget, we've discussed the subject. I know everything about your stomach pains. I gave you the wins to finance the surgery you're going to need."

"So?"

"See you in hospital."

"What?"

But the voice was gone.

Jenna had been by his bedside for 48 hours, and the doctor had said, there was nothing more could be done. She must get some rest. She'd been crying and her eyes were red rimmed. Bryce had already survived longer than anyone had predicted. He was a fighter, but the cancer had been widespread. She got up to leave, and stood gazing over him for several moments. Bryce looked ashen, his face lined and weary; he shifted restlessly from side to side, unable to find peace. Then she walked out quietly with the doctor, a young Puerto Rican gentleman, who said, softly, "He's still with us. He's young and he's strong. He might yet pull through."

"I thought she'd never go," said the voice.

"You again?"

"Me again."

"Leave me alone. I'm dying."

"How about one last bet then?"

"You have to be joking."

"Humour me. You're already pretty much gone."

The hospital equipment was flat-lining, soundlessly.

"See, I can bring you back. You're not beyond recall."

"What do you want?"

"You said you'd bet your life we all die one day. You're dead now. Your heart's stopped. But what if I have the elixir of life, to bring you back? You lose your bet, but I give you life. Not eternal, but for now."

"How do you do that?"

"Look!" Bryce saw a glass of clear liquid within reach. "Drink," said the voice. And Bryce drank, greedily. Clutching at life. Drinking it in. A glorious feeling of health and elation. The hospital equipment sprang back into life. "See, I told you," said the voice. "I have the elixir of life. I said you should trust me; that I'm much misunderstood."

"So I'm back in the land of the living?" said Bryce. "Wonderful."

"Ah, but there's a catch, I'm afraid. I do tend to cheat sometimes. It's so much more fun. You see, sadly, in winning your bet; you lose your life, precisely because I've brought you back. You must understand, you bet your life. And that's what you must now forfeit. Sorry about that. C'est la vie," the voice smirked. "Or should I say, c'est la mort?"

"You're talking rubbish, my friend. I've won. Don't *you* see, I'm alive. You've just let me win. Idiot! You lose." Thank God, he thought. Jenna would be overjoyed. She'd always wanted to do a long cruise, one of those that combines an African safari. Bryce felt that happy flurry of expectation. It was just so good to be alive. The dreams were no more than that; just dreams. How could he have been fooled by thinking they were anything else. He settled his head back into the delicious duck down pillow, and slumbered long and deeply for the first time in months.

The white coated man was a stranger in the hospital, but no-one thought to accost him. He stood over Bryce, frowning down at him angrily as the life preserving equipment purred on steadily. Bryce slept peacefully. Dreamed of his darling Jenna. Nothing could touch him now. He was safe. Safe at last.

"Arrogant bastard," the man muttered, flipping a switch on the life support which went into immediate arrest. "Won your bet, didn't you," he murmured. "Lost your life."

Chapter Three

THE KNOCKING

*T*he detective thought he might be sick, but swallowed back the ripple of bile that threatened to choke him. The image was one that would remain with him for the rest of his life.

The scene was one of desperate carnage.

The stench, oily, metallic and excremental.

The room, in curtained semi-darkness despite its being midday and sunny outside.

The sight; blood, pooled, puddled and splashed; shit smeared and an impenetrable casserole of shredded human flesh, hanging electric wires and circuits, shattered screens, keyboards and consoles. Added to that were jagged splinters of smashed furniture, broken glass, torn up carpet and ceiling light fittings wrenched from their moorings. There was still some phantom sense of movement in the room, as though things dead had aspects of them continuing to breath and survive. Exposed cables flickered, flashed and showered firework sparks; one of the computer screens shimmered with a jigsaw of indeterminate flaring images in both black and white and colour. There was a muffled hum from something electrical, like a swarm of bees buzzing around the place.

He had a vision from some old film of explorers in tropical heat having to cut through jungle with machetes, and thought the same approach might produce a comparable result here.

You couldn't walk round it, or through it. There was no way but to clamber over it, the pile of inanimate and corporeal rubble, and he'd leave that treat to Scene of Crime.

Detective Chief Inspector, Michael Filbert thought about the moments, early this morning before the call had come in. Moments when he'd put out the coco pops for four year old twins, Daisy and Bella before stirring in the porridge he and his wife Freddy would enjoy. A chill morning helped by a hot breakfast, at least for two of the family.

Then the call had come. A sombre voice. A spooked whisper. 'Better get out here quick Gov. It's a multiple. Never seen anything like it.

Now Filbert stood surrounded by, he knew not what. Never in all his career in the force had he encountered anything like it. He looked as though he had no idea where to start. An accurate assessment of his present state of mind.

A YEAR ago her children had persuaded ninety-four year old, white haired Granny Pickles, loved by all, but who could be sharp as well as she could be sweet, to go into a care home. The family were well off, so it was agreed she could move into a compact private house rather than one of those larger places populated by hundreds of residents, the thought of which, at her time of life, she found frankly terrifying.

The staff were full-time domestic, but it had to be explained to Granny that the team were an amalgam of human and cyborg. The idea left her bewildered. 'There'll generally be three daytime and three for nights,' her son Matthew had reassured her. A tall slim gentleman, with distinctive copper coloured hair, he had a soft spoken manner, 'And there'll be a further half dozen back-up for when the regulars get their time off.'

'How will I get to remember all their names,' Granny had quavered. 'And will they know I like salt on my porridge in the morning, and nutmeg in my apple pie, and on lamb chops?' She'd started to cry.

Matt leaned over his mother, a hand on her shoulder, 'Mum, don't be silly. These people are all there to help you. We'll tell them everything you want and everything you need; foods, medicines, films, books, clothing, outings to parks and drives to the seaside for candyfloss, ice creams and rock. And,' he paused, 'They're all medically qualified too.'

'What, even the mechanical ones?' she'd protested.

'Absolutely. And, if we don't tell you which are the cyborgs you'll never know. They're impossible to distinguish from human beings. Really,' he sounded animated. 'They're intelligent, they're soft and warm and friendly, and yes, let me emphasise again, all of them are medically qualified. This is 2060 mum, not 1966 when you were born. Also, don't forget that we'll be there to visit you regularly, with the kids and the rest of the family from time to time. I promise you, you'll love it.'

From the comfortable armchair, she looked at her daughter-in-law, 'Meg, darling. What do you think? Will I be alright there?'

Primping her greying hair, rosy cheeked Meg looked down at her petite in-law, 'You'll be fine Ma. Honestly. We'll come with you to the place, see you settled in.'

'Cyborgs? the old lady wailed.

'You can't stay here on your own any more, mum, said Matt. 'Too many mishaps, falls, taps left running. Goodness, you nearly burned the place down when you left the gas on. God,' he pondered, 'You might have blown the place up. It's got to be full time, mum, round the clock.'

Granny sat with her head in her hands, 'Robots? I really don't know. I'm not sure I can. If they're not human, some of them.'

'Ma, you won't know the difference,' cut in Meg again. 'Even they don't, and won't always know the difference, if no-one tells them. When a cyborg meets and recognises an ordinary human being they refer to us as antiques, as though they're the future and we're the past. They're absolutely fantastic. Unbelievable. Only the agency supplying them will know for sure. They can do absolutely anything these days, trust me. You'll have a free choice in type, you can even choose the gender, race, hair colour, age, political opinions, taste in books and music. Darling, if you want a Jewish male robot? we'll get the agency to show you he's circumcised if you think it'll help. But it'll work better if nobody knows which are human and which are not.'

'What if they're dangerous? What if they get out of control?'

'They're okay Gran,' chimed in Timmy, her eight year old grandson.'

Gran looked at him and his sister fondly, she'd been all of 42 when she'd had Matty, and he'd been 44 when Timmy was born, with his father's copper coloured hair, and 48 when 6 year old, blond curly Babs arrived.

She asked him, 'Are they okay my pet?'

'Yes Gran,' said Timmy, eagerly attempting to clamber up on to his Grandmother's knee, while his mother gently dissuaded him, pointing out his granny's age and frailty. 'You see,' Timmy went on, daddy told me about the robot's code of conduct.'

Gran Pickles looked enquiringly at her son.

'That's right mum. I'll recite them to you, now and then we'll post it on all the walls of the house so you can remind yourself if you ever get slightly nervous. Are you listening?'

She nodded, and her son went on,

> 1. ' A robot may not injure a human being or, through
>   inaction, allow a human being to come to harm.

'Well that's a relief,' said Gran. 'After all…'
'Hang on a sec mum,' Matty looked intent.

> 2. A robot must obey the orders given it by human
>   beings except where such orders would conflict with
>   the First Law.

> *'I think I see what that means,' she offered.*
> *'Finally,' Matt sounded more sure of himself.*
> 3. A robot must protect its own existence as long as such
>   protection does not conflict with the First or Second
>   Laws.

Before Matt could add anything further, Timmy, her eight year old grandson put in again, 'Daddy, when you visit Granny, can we come too?'

And so Granny Pickles had settled in to the home and found herself getting used to the robots looking after her despite, or perhaps benefitting from not knowing for sure which were real and which were not.

The family religiously visited the old lady once a month when the staff would have tea and cakes laid out and waiting for them. It was lovely. Gran flourished there, the family remarking on the fact that over the months she looked well, fit and if anything younger than her years. Certainly much better than when she'd first gone to the house when she'd looked fragile, frightened and bewildered.

What Granny had not been told was that rather than a mix of human and cyborg, Matthew and Meg had agreed that all the helpers should be cyborg. Cyborg would be consistent in their patterns of behaviour, attitude, treatment of Gran, and so on. Humans, with the best will in the world, would be unpredictable, inconsistent and subject to the usual household politics of bickering, petty jealousies and infantile bullying as helpers jockeyed for ascendancy.

Matty and his wife had keys, but out of respect for his mother they always knocked before entering the house on visiting days.

Tap tap, they'd go, and wait for the gently quavering but jubilant, 'Who's there?'

'It's us Granny,' Timmy and Babs would shout, to which the reply, 'Come in now darlings.' The family would spend the afternoon with Granny, the cyborgs cheerfully serving up tea and cucumber sandwiches followed by scones, clotted cream with jam and finally delicious cyborg made cream cakes.

Gran had been comfortably ensconced in the house for some months when Timmy remarked one afternoon while they were driving home, that one of the cyborgs had a bruise on his forearm. 'I thought that cyborgs weren't supposed to bruise?' he asked.

What none of the family had heard from the confines of the car over the sound of its engine, had been the piercing scream that had issued from the house just after they'd left. A passer-by had been stopped in his tracks, looked around puzzled, for the source of the cry, and then hearing nothing further had merely shrugged and walked on.

Meg turned to look round at Timmy from the front seat of the car, 'They don't darling. It might have been a smudge of dirt you saw.'

Timmy put on one of his sceptical looks, 'Looked like a bruise to me,' he muttered.

On another occasion Matthew himself was aware of something odd, but said nothing to anyone. One of the cyborgs, Jed, Matt thought, had confided that a red headed female cyborg called Joyce had been flirting with one of the replacement staff, a good looking guy called Ivan. Matt was beginning to suspect that some antiques, like him had been introduced into the house, though he couldn't be sure. The robots were safe to be with, and Gran was in no danger, but still, the thought that something had been going on over which he had neither control nor knowledge, troubled him.

Still more mystifying, when one of the original cyborgs, a big fellow with jug-ears named Gus, leaned over to give Matt a cup of tea, he couldn't help noticing that Gus had slightly bad breath and a smell of perspiration. Matthew and Meg had been specific at the robot distribution centre; no human staff, only cyborgs, and cyborgs didn't have body odours.

Timmy heard the scream next, again as they left the house and were getting into the car. A drawn out animal howl. An overcast late afternoon. Granny had seemed distracted. The cyborg helpers ill at ease. An odd atmosphere over tea, only perceived by Timmy, his fears for Granny immediately discounted by Mum as they drove off. 'Come on Timmy,' she smiled reassuringly, 'If Gran had a problem she'd have told us, wouldn't she darling?'

Then Dad had added, 'And cyborgs don't scream Timmy.'

But Timmy, frowning, remained unconvinced.

In the home one of the daytime helpers, Jed, looked anxiously at Granny, 'What was all that about then?' he enquired kindly. 'If your family heard that they'd be worried sick.'

'I suddenly got anxious when they'd gone,' the old lady said. 'I felt terribly alone. Sometimes none of this seems real.' She was sitting in the same armchair the family had left her in when they'd departed. The tea things hadn't yet been cleared away. 'I mean, are all of you real?' she whimpered. 'Or are you all robots or something? It's all getting so complicated.'

Running his fingers through his luxuriant dark hair, Jed gently responded, 'You know we're all real Mrs…'

'Oh do call me Gran,' she protested. 'All this Mr and Mrs, it's so mechanical. No warmth.'

'Of course, Gran,' said Jed. 'Not a problem.' The helper started to collect the remains of sandwiches and small cakes, shoving them onto a tray to remove them to the kitchen. With Ivan working the garden, the other two helpers could be heard moving about apparently changing bedsheets upstairs, and their tread became louder as they descended the flight.

The three staff now faced Granny. Jed, Gus and Joyce. It looked as though some sort of decision had been made. 'Time we had a talk old lady,' said Joyce, her hands shoved in the pockets of her jeans, her white blouse almost insolently open at the neck. 'All this fuss and bother. Don't want you disturbing the neighbours now do we. So don't be a silly Granny,' she added softly. 'Or we may have to switch you off for a while. Or maybe switch you off for good? Can't have you screaming and worrying people all the time. Won't do at all.'

'What do you mean,' wailed Granny, now rigid with fear. 'Switch me off? Switch me off? I'm not a robot., Don't think I don't know what's been going on here, it's *you* who're robots. Not me. I wanted real people for carers. I don't know what's happened. Where's my Matty? Why's he left me like this?'

'Well now, is that how you see it Granny?' Joyce stood over Granny, sweeping her red hair aside with a flick of her head. 'Then let me enlighten you old lady.'

Granny bowed her head, grasping it with both hands, 'I'm not sure I really want to hear this, do I?'

'You tell me dear. You don't have to hear anything if you don't want to.' Joyce paused, grinning slightly at the old lady's discomfiture.

'Very well,' she responded, 'If you must.' Granny felt her heart

battering against her ribs. I shouldn't be subjected to this sort of thing, she thought, not at my age. It simply isn't fair.

Ivan had come in from the garden in his big rubber boots and blue dungarees and was brushing bits of soil from his palms, having propped the small axe he'd been using against one leg. Granny resisted the temptation to berate him for the mess, and looked at Joyce. She felt very small and very scared. Were these helpers really all robots as Matthew had promised? They all looked and sounded so very real. But then, robots didn't sneer and laugh at you the way Joyce had. Then she held her breath and waited for Joyce to continue.

'Sorry to disappoint you darling, but I have to tell you...'

'Yes, yes. Tell me what? For heaven's sake, will you please hurry.'

'You're a droid darling.'

'A what? A droid? What the dickens is a droid?'

'Well, not strictly droid, but cyborg, to be precise.'

'Please, this is all too confusing. Droid? Cyborg? Robot? Am I going insane?' She was starting to cry now, shivering and shaking with fear.

Joyce glanced at the other three who just stood around looking embarrassed. Then she crouched down in front of Granny, 'Listen to me darling. Your predecessor was the real Granny.'

'Predecessor? Predecessor? What predecessor? Impossible. I don't know what you're talking about. Oh, this is becoming an absolute nightmare,' the old lady sobbed. 'I wish Matty had never...'

'But she didn't like being attended by robots,' Joyce interrupted. 'So she got in in touch with the agency and had them send her some real people. What we call antiques.'

'But I'm an antique. Matty told me we're all antiques. You're telling me I'm a robot? I simply don't believe it.'

'Will you let me finish,' the other sighed. 'Granny; that's the real Granny, drove the antique carers nuts. Never stopped bellyaching and complaining. She wasn't the lovely old dear her family know. Seems Granny Pickles raised their hackles. In fact she was a bloody tyrant, subject to unpredictable bouts of rage. Left the carers quite alarmed, even frightened at times. Frightened of a little old lady. Just think of it.'

Joyce paused for a moment and smirked. 'So they did a naughty and paid the agency a small fortune to have the real Granny disappear and replaced with you. Actually, they killed her, the genuine one. Bit messy, but hey, it cleared up. You'd never know. Family never suspected a thing. Got rid of the traces of blood with bleach. And anyway, no-one reported a dead Granny. So no problem. Yep? Then they had a party to celebrate when you arrived.' Joyce sat back on her heels and laughed. 'Can you believe it? You're so good, not even you know you're a cyborg. Trouble is, when they manufactured you, with all the old Granny Pickles memories and characteristics, it seems the bad temper came with it.'

'How can I not know?' she protested. 'If what you say is true of course I must know. And I am not a cyborg.'

''Fraid you are darling. See something went wrong when they were delivering you here. You were dropped, or something. Banged your head,' Joyce looked at the others, idly standing around, who nodded their agreement. 'But then see,' she went on, 'You were a very bad girl. Because you kept getting angry. Just like the one they'd got rid of. Only worse. And you kept forgetting things. Didn't you?'

'I don't know. Did I?'

'Obviously. You don't remember *now*, do you? You've forgotten that the original version of you replaced the cyborg staff with antiques.'

The old lady remained mute. She just looked at the carers with mounting alarm. The whole thing was clearly a very nasty joke. 'Is that it then?' she asked, at last beginning to feel extremely annoyed.

'No it's not. Because then, horror of horrors, while they were sleeping one night, you went round to their beds and strangled them, one by one.'

'What?'

'That's right. But the agency still didn't want to lose the income they were getting from your son. So they replaced the dead carers with new ones.'

'All of you?'

'All of us. You finally latched on Gran.'

'And you're real people?'

'That's us.'

'More real people?'

'Right on.'

'To replace the last lot of real people you say I killed?'

'Correct.'

'Antiques?'

'Don't knock it baby. Cyborgs are great for filling in, doing the donkey work. Odd jobs. But they're not the real McCoy.'

'I suppose you're the real McCoy.'

'World revolves around us, dear. Not you. We can live without you. You can't live without us.'

'If you say so,' Granny whispered. 'I suppose I shall simply have to get used to the idea that I'm not an antique.' She pondered for a few moments, then asked, 'If I killed the last set of carers, as you claim, and about whom I have no recollection, aren't you all afraid of what I might do to you?'

'No dear,' said Joyce. 'We keep a close eye on you. Won't happen again, not on our watch.' The others nodded their assent again. 'We, or the night team sleep in relays. This job pays too much to walk away from. No more stranglings in the night though, old lady. And if you tried anything, well, just look at you. Up against these three blokes? Don't make me laugh.'

Granny felt as confused as ever. But of one thing she was absolutely certain. Irrespective of what Joyce was saying. She was human, of course she was. A cyborg wouldn't question its own existence in this way. As for killing the earlier carers. Nonsense. But then what were these people up to?

She would have to get in touch with the agency herself. She had their number somewhere. In fact, she could remember it. Quite clearly. And Matty's mobile, and business number, come to think of it. Meg's too. And their home landline. No problem. Of course she hadn't banged her head. But she mustn't worry her son. She'd simply get on with things herself.

It was in that instant she had a moment of clarity. A calming sense of overwhelming relief. Knowledge was always king, wasn't it. These people weren't antiques at all, they were cyborgs. Of course, they were. All of them. Trying to control her by seeking to convince her she was a robot. She smiled to herself and shook her head pityingly at the thought. Well, she wasn't about to be fooled. Not now. Not ever. Too long in the tooth for that sort of thing. She sighed. Comforted at last.

A week later her loved ones came round. Eagerly anticipated. Gran had actually gone to the trouble of preparing the tea herself. Cucumber sandwiches with the crusts cut off. Home made scones. She loved baking. Clotted cream ordered in, together with a selection of cream cakes. Everything laid out on the big mahogany table in the living room. A veritable banquet. She was happy; only a small indefinable cloud of disquiet marred her horizon. Something not quite right she couldn't identify. Somewhat untidy everywhere despite her best efforts to make everything neat and ship-shape. No help from the staff today, it seemed. Nagging headache as well. Ho hum, she thought. Best get on with things.

Tap tap, went the front door. 'Who's there,' came the old lady's joyful response.

'It's us Gran,' cried Timmy as he flung into the room.

Matty looked amazed. No helpers in sight. 'My my, Ma. Bit of a mess in here? Curtains drawn? I mean it's sunny out. But what a spread. And you've done it all on your own?' Then he saw the pools of blood, and broken furniture, his neck felt wet and the room went dark.

Then Meg, looking around said, 'Oh no Ma! Please no!' It was the last thing she said as she saw her children, Timmy and Babs, lying at her feet with their throats slit.

'Thought you could fool me did you?' the old lady snarled, now becoming focused. Told me they were all people when they were really robots. Antiques!' she snorted. 'Well, I'm not an antique, but they are,' she pointed at the partially hidden bodies piled behind and among crackling wires of broken computers that no-one had had time to take in. 'This lot. I'm a human being, not a blinking antique. Replaced the robots with real people, didn't I. The agency was only too willing to help, as long as Matty was paying.'

The sepia image of a timid old lady sipping from a mug of tea, surrounded by family, flickered before her eyes. She felt troubled by the sight. Then it was gone. But the anger remained.

'Then they told me, the real ones, this crowd, that I was a droid. But there were others before these, they said. What happened to *them* is what I want to know? Can't remember. Banged my head on delivery, so wasn't aware. Couldn't believe it. And they laughed at me. No-one laughs at Granny, she growled, waving Timmy's paper detailing the Robot's code. Except they got one thing totally wrong. I'm not a cyborg. I'm Granny Pickles. Only they weren't smart enough to figure that out. Where's my Matty? I want my boy,' she shrieked as she brought the axe down on Meg's head.

DI FILBERT STOOD amid the wreck of machinery and humanity. 'Who reported this? He asked tiredly.

'Neighbour reported hearing screams, Gov. And this what we found.'

'Poor old dear,' Filbert looked down at the old lady slumped on the floor with her back against the wall, a bloodied breadknife and a small pickaxe nearby. 'Who could have done this to her? Cut her throat? For God's sake. Harmless old thing. Probably never hurt a fly. And who or what are these?' He indicated the bodies and bits of bodies that littered the floor.

'Dunno Gov. Looks like a bloody civil war. Bodies, machines, furniture, all smashed up.'

Reaching down DI Filbert took a crumpled piece of paper the old lady still had within her grasp, then he looked up, perplexed. 'It says here, "A robot may not injure a human being or, through inaction, allow a human being to come to harm."' Looking down at Granny Pickles, he went on, 'But this old lady isn't a robot, and no-one could mistake her for one.' Filbert bent down to take a closer look at Granny. Then he looked at the paper again.

Straightening up he turned to his sergeant, saying softly, 'You know I think I may be wrong. I do believe she's killed everyone here.'

'What? How could she? She's outnumbered. She's weak and frail. Her throat's been cut. How could she have done it Gov? For a start she'd never be strong enough.'

'Yes she would sergeant. You see, *she* was the robot, and the robots can be made to appear like anything the manufacturers choose; young, old, beautiful, ugly. But they're all machines in the end, and strong as steel, no matter what they look like. She'd have had no trouble dealing with this lot. There's clearly been a catastrophic event here. We may never know what. But she's evidently contravened the robot's protocol as outlined on this,' he held up the paper. And my God, she must have been raging. Gone berserk. Looks as though cyborgs do have feelings after all.

'But Gov, if she's killed everyone here, literally slaughtered them, and she's too strong for the lot of them, then who's killed her?'

'Obvious, isn't it sarge. When you contravene the code you can't be allowed to live. She knew that, so she was left with no choice but to kill herself. Knowing how close the manufacturers made their cyborgs to resemble and mimic a human being it was a fair bet she'd die if she slit her own throat. And she was right.'

Chapter Four

PREDATORS

*T*he chick would be up later; right now he was busy. He'd asked for the same one as yesterday, the chunky little black one with the tight ass and small tits. He'd hit her, slapped her round the face, made her lip bleed, shown her who was boss. And she'd hit him back, spat in his face. He couldn't believe it; in all his life no hooker had ever dared. Funny thing was, it'd given him a hard on. So she was going to have to learn a lesson, little Miss.

Ten years ago there'd been something similar, a near scandal. Silly bitch had screamed the place down; spent a month in hospital. Cost him a fortune, having her broken jaw wired up, her nose reset, and then the cosmetic surgery. Jesus! Avoiding publicity had cost another fortune. His knuckles had remained bruised for a week; but it was worth it for the high it gave him. He'd jerked off twice a day for the week with the memory of it. One day it wouldn't be enough for him. But for now!

On the seventeenth floor, in the penthouse suite of the Quin Hotel on West 37th Street, close by New York's Fifth Avenue, Gilbert Vansittart sank back into the soft confines of the luxury armchair, cradled within the muted lighting of his luxury accommodation and sipped from his leaded cut glass, a

Macallan No 6. 1824 series, malt whisky. At more than $4,000 a bottle, with its apple and clove nose, and its cinnamon and ginger palate, it was well-nigh matchless. But then Vansittart's skills were well-nigh matchless, and he'd more than earned life's little pleasures. He'd travelled to New York from his home in Washington to be present when his organisation, the multi-billion dollar, Vansittart Corporation, took over the rather smaller, Pacific Oriental Corporation, whilst destroying Its Chief Executive Officer, its CEO, the gentle and mild mannered, Jeremy, (Jenny), Wren.

Wren had built his organisation with the help of loyal and talented staff over a twenty-year period, trading in commodities, real estate and IT. They were like an extended family and operated as a team.

Vansittart had built his empire pretty much alone, swallowing smaller, weaker organisations along the way, spitting out their CEOs, and enjoying every minute of it. Survival of the fittest, was his motto. Survival of the ruthless. No room on this planet for the weak. In Vansittart's eyes, kindness represented weakness and had to be stamped on at all costs. In the next few days little Jenny Wren would learn all about Charles Darwin in what would prove to be an object lesson in the 19th century scientist's treatise on evolution. Kill or be killed. Eat or be eaten.

There was a knock at the door to Vansittart's suite and two immaculately uniformed hotel staff trundled in a massive, wheeled trolley with pristine white cloth, covering a five-course meal.

"Out," shouted Vansittart; the big man lumbering to his feet, his belly overhanging his trousers, shirt collar twisted, sleeves undone at the cuff, thick black hair awry. "You're two minutes late. When I say 10.00 pm I mean 10.00 pm, not 10.02." Vansittart's pulse was up and he was sweating underarm and beneath the rolls of stomach fat. He sensed a fight as his view narrowed on the two who'd just entered his suite. Innocent youngsters, trying to do a job of work. A couple of life's losers. He smiled inwardly. Any prospect of a fight, an argument or dispute, and Vansittart would be there. At school he'd cheated his way to becoming heavyweight boxing champion, treading on opponents' toes and punching low whenever the referee was unsighted. Several times he'd come close to disqualification, but always protested his innocence, on one occasion even feigning tears, despite topping 6 feet 4 inches and weighing over 250 pounds. His shirt was sticking to him now as perspiration leaked down his back and front.

"Sir," said one of the two young men, tall and slender with floppy blond hair, "It is actually just 9.58 right now. We're okay for time!"

"Son," said Vansittart stumbling towards the young men, his bloodshot eyes, red veined ping pong balls, "when I say it's 10.02 it's 10.02. I don't care if the fucking clock in Grand Central says four in the fucking afternoon. You got that kid?"

"Y, Yes Sir!"

"Now take the fucking food away, son, before I throw it and your fucking trolley down the fucking lift shaft. Comprendé?" As the two men hurriedly exited the suite with the trolley in tow, they heard Vansittart on the hotel's phone, "When's the fucking food coming? How long am I s'posed to wait in this chicken shit, motel?"

Descended from the English Vansittarts, a cousin several times removed, the 1st Baron, Lord Robert Vansittart had been Permanent Under-Secretary for Foreign Affairs to the Prime Minister in the pre-World War II period 1930 to 1938, and a senior, British diplomat in the period up to 1941. He is best remembered for his opposition to Appeasement and his hard-line stance towards Germany during and after the Second World War. He was also a highly cultured individual, being a published poet, novelist and playwright. He was a man who combined a brilliant mind with an uncompromising approach towards his enemies, of whom the principal one was Germany. Not surprisingly, among friends and close associates, despite his diplomatic credentials, he was known as, 'The killer.'

In business, Vansittart had inherited all of his cousin's killer instincts, but in other respects, fell somewhat short on his diplomatic talents and reputed integrity.

Jenny Wren was working late, with his staff. They knew Vansittart was in town, and Wren's number two and number three were alarmed. Wren's number two, Edrich Johns, a Certified Public Accountant with flame red hair and freckled cheeks, said, "Jen, he's been buying up our stock all day. Where does he get the cash from? He's asset rich, but all his trading is suffering from cash flow deficiencies. At this rate he'll have us under his belt in less than 48 hours."

Frank Esterhauzer, Wren's number three, a lawyer with more than 30 years in the profession of corporate law, eased his lanky frame out of the easy chair and wandered around Wren's office as though searching for something. "What's he up to Jen? He doesn't need to be doing this.

Wren sighed, running his hands through thinning light brown hair. He was a small man, with an almost feminine voice, stocky, and narrow shouldered, a pink complexion and a permanently puzzled expression. As if he wasn't really sure what the world was about, nor what his place in it was supposed to be. "He's borrowing, more than he can afford to service in debt, taking out options, selling all his deadwood for whatever he can get. The man's on a mission. He'll work through the night, with assets to dispose of in dozens of different time zones, he'll be raising the cash to buy us out."

THE AFRICAN SUN beat down raising the temperature to close on 35 degrees Celsius. She surveyed the landscape, her young, starving at her feet, mewling piteously. One, an undersized cub, was probably already close to death. It couldn't be more than hours. Maybe no more than an hour. She'd lost all of her previous litter to starvation and didn't want a repeat. The males were away hunting in a group, but she preferred to hunt alone. She had only the thinnest memory of the last time she'd felt sated, her belly bulging with kill.

The gazelle were not far distant, the sight of them made her mouth water. She sniffed the air, kept herself upwind of the herd and padded softly in a wide arc, staying out of sight, ducking down, practically crawling through the sparse dry brown vegetation. She was running dangerously short of time, and she more than sensed it.

———

THE HUNTER, accompanied by two park rangers, a tracker and a guide had been chasing spoor all day under the scorching sun. He was a tall man, in his fifties, with curly grey hair and a 60's Zapata moustache. They'd found elephant dung, and from the size of the accompanying footprints, appear to have been tracking a small group of sizeable males. He wasn't interested in the ivory; the kill was what excited him. So far, the group had only caught occasional sight of the herd as they moved almost silently through the thick brush, losing them, then finding them again when the low rumble of their feeding, or the cracking of branches told the group of men where they were.

He was sweating profusely. Bull elephants were one of the biggest challenges a hunter could take on; intelligent, protective of their females and their young; they could be terrifyingly fierce. Eight tons of slate grey mountain, thirteen feet at the shoulder, bearing down on you at 25 mph, head doubled in size by batwing ears, trunk roiling and trumpeting, wild eyes raging; it needed a cool head to lift the rifle and aim at the vulnerable areas of the creature. The .400 calibre he carried was heavy, but accurate. It needed to be, as he'd have to fire from close up. The killing shots couldn't be delivered from a distance with any chance of absolute accuracy, or indeed any chance of penetrating the armour-plated hide. Every year hunters died trying to bring down an elephant. He knew there'd be no second chances, no reruns. And anyway, it wasn't the hide he was going to be aiming at, it was the skull shot. Man on man; man on bull. Dangerous, orgasmic. Unrepeatable. The thought of it made his scalp prickle. They were aggressive bastards, bush elephants, and they didn't much like men. Bit like some of the women he knew.

He wiped the back of his neck with a grimy kerchief and, undoing his flies urinated noisily against a tree. Okay, so bush elephants could be killers, but then, so was he. He grinned to himself, the moustache curling up in a wide parabola.

His wealth was inherited, or at least the business upon which his wealth was based was inherited; a number of giant cash and carry type stores selling just about anything and everything, from food and clothes to electrical goods. In fact, he'd not done particularly well. Blissfully unaware he lacked both judgement and business acumen, when the old man had passed the running of the business on to him he'd practically run it into the ground. He'd had to bring in his brother, little bro' Sim, who'd set the thing back on its feet again, while he, older brother, Henry, had contrived to take all the credit.

Henry was going to bring down a big one. Little lady back at the camp would be mightily impressed. Elephant, he pondered; the most exciting hunting known to man. Man being the operative word in Henry's mind. Not a sport for women. Women, like his new girlfriend, Marietta, thirty years his junior, and pretty insatiable, were meant to be to be subordinate to men. Alright; so he hadn't been that impressive in the sack. Two ex-wives had made the same complaint. They'd gone so far as to compare notes. But he'd shortly make that up with a large kill. Then maybe Etta would stop making eyes at some of the younger guys in the group. Etta with her Mexican complexion, her long black hair and flashing eyes. That flimsy cotton top she wore, with half the buttons undone, was driving the men nuts. For a moment he wondered what she might be up to while he was away; but he dismissed the thought. He was her man, no doubt about it. Not much in the sack? We'd soon see little lady; we'd soon see.

IT WAS midday in New York, and Vansittart had more than thirty percent of Pacific Oriental Corporation under his control. It was going well, like he'd known it would. As Wren had predicted Vansittart had worked through the night. By the end of the day POC would be his, and Mr Wren would be history. Wren was probably wondering how Vansittart could possibly be finding the funds to layout in this takeover bid. It was easy; so easy it made him laugh out loud.

In the offices of POC, Edrich Johns took a call from Jenny's wife, Susan. "How's it looking, Ed?" she asked, hesitantly.

"Not good," he muttered, reaching for the nearly cold black coffee on his desk. He took a sip, then stretched, and rubbed the back of his stiffening neck. It had been a long night for all of them. The day was turning out much longer.

"How's Jen bearing up?"

"Oh you know Jen; never lets on he's worried.

"But we could end up ruined, yes? If Jen tries to fight the takeover and commits funds we don't have?"

"I know Sue, I know. We'll just have to play it by ear. Look, I'm not pretending it's going to be easy, but right now I really don't know how things're going to pan out."

Vansittart smiled to himself, poured another scalding black coffee from the cafetiere, added in some of the $4,000 malt, took a gulp, belched loudly and sat back feeling eminently satisfied. The sun shone into his suite, another glorious New York day. The gods were on his side. Weren't they always? So what if he was short of the readies? What the hell! Gilbert Vansittart wasn't about to let a little thing like a lack of funds slow his progress, he'd built his business with a lack of funds, taking risks, and, more importantly using the assets of the companies he was proposing to take over as collateral for his loans. Sure, he hadn't necessarily always been in a strong position to take over the companies he was after at that particular early stage, but with the bids he was putting in the lenders, those investors who had absolute faith in him, would be prepared to lend to him on a promise. And if the takeover didn't succeed he'd give them the collateral of his own corporate assets to keep them happy. It was so beautiful; you took over a company, paid nothing and did it all on borrowed funds secured on the prey's own assets. Beautiful.

———

SHE WAS EXHAUSTED, her first two attempts having failed, and she needed to rest. She was fast, very fast, up to 70 miles per hour, but only for short bursts. The Thompson's gazelle weren't quite as fast, but they were agile and could maintain the pace for longer. Her body ached and she was weakening for lack of food. What was worse, the cub, the one in trouble, wouldn't survive much longer. They were both into borrowed time, not unfamiliar territory, but death stalked the hunter as much as the hunter stalked her prey. She might have the energy for one final attempt, but even as she planned it, she sank to the ground, unable to move.

———

"PUT ME THROUGH TO JEN, ED," said Susan.

"Are you sure?"

"Just put me through." Susan's background was as modest as had been her husband's, and she was a cautious woman who'd admired her husband and his successes more than she could possibly say. Petite and dumpy, with mousey brown hair, and a somewhat outdated sense of fashion, she'd been a kindergarten teacher before marrying Jeremy. It had taken her a long time to conceive, at first, something to do with Jen's sperm count; then she'd had two more in quick succession. Now with three children under the age of ten, she was a full-time housewife. Her father, a minister in the local protestant church, had preached thrift, and despite the wealth of POC, she was an insecure woman, ever afraid that her husband's perceived risk taking in business might one day be his undoing. "What's happening, Jen?" she asked.

"Vansittart!!"

"God! That man! What does he want, for heaven's sake?"

"My throat, Sue. It's not the money he's after. He's got all he could possibly need. It's the hunt and it's the kill that are his big turn on."

"But Jen, we don't need the money either. Aren't we rich enough?"

There was a long silence, then Wren said, "Sue, honey, we live well within our means. That's not the point. The bigger the outfit the bigger the risks. Enron might have been a vast criminal web, but even its wealth couldn't save it from disaster."

"But, we're not criminal." She sounded hesitant.

"Of course we're not. I'm just making a point that any organisation can be vulnerable to the unforeseen, the unpredicted. If we were taken over I don't know where that would leave us."

"What's the worst that could happen, Jen?"

"Really?"

"Really!"

We could find ourselves out on our necks. I'm too old to get a job, and though the stocks are worth a fortune; yes we're rich; I don't know how Vansittart might manipulate the stock price, once he gained control, to push it down, buying me out for a song, and securing the whole shooting match."

"Jen," she softly, "I'm frightened."

"Don't be," Wren said. But he didn't sound that sure. He hung up, felt a chill in his bones, as Ed and Frank were hovering, wandering disconsolately around his office, ties loose, shirts-sleeves rolled to the elbow, phones to their ears, eyes to the several screens in Wren's office. "He's up to 40 percent, Jen," said Frank. We're being eaten alive." Frank, the corporate lawyer, bull necked, broad shouldered, had been with Wren through thick and thin over the years, each man advising, encouraging and supporting the other.

"Back in a second," said Wren, as he walked out of his office, leaving the other two on their own.

Wren had been born in the tiny Midwest town of Zoar, Ohio. First settled in 1817 by German religious separatists who believed hard work led to salvation, Wren's father, a bookkeeper, had wholeheartedly subscribed to the philosophy and saw to it that his son did too, working him twelve to fourteen hours a day when he was at school in Cleveland, some 75 miles away, to where they'd removed when the boy was five years old. He was undersized for his age, not into sports or other masculine pursuits, yet despite being ripe for bullying, it never happened. His risqué sense of humour and willingness to help others less academically gifted made him one of the most popular of his year. Unsurprisingly the lad had done well, earning himself a scholarship to Yale where he studied law, qualifying summa cum laud. His mother, a shy and retiring woman, had worked in the local general store at Zoar until they removed to Cleveland where-after she concentrated on added home tuition to help her son pre-university. After leaving university Wren took an evening course in accountancy, duly qualifying as a Certified Public Accountant. He was a natural talent at whatever he turned his hand to, easily picking up IT, even going so far as to design software he sold to various IT companies. That was his launching pad, it went on to involve building computers, selling them at first to individual business people, then larger corporations and then moving on to expand into a whole range of businesses including property in the States and the Far East, tie ups with computer companies in South Korea, China and Japan, whilst simultaneously dabbling, then dealing on a vast scale with commodities such as grains, oil, natural gas, coffee, copper and gold. POC was a mega organisation, but still not as huge as the hungry predator that comprised Vansittart's group.

"He's frightened," said Frank. "I've never seen him like this; but Jen's scared. What do we do? What's he doing to stop Vansittart?"

Ed frowned, shrugged, "I don't know Frank. But if Jen can't pull the fat out of the fire, no-one can. Thing is, Vansittart's big, bigger than us. We never ever planned on anything like this happening. Maybe we should have. But you know as well as I do, you can't plan for everything."

THE HERD WERE RESTIVE, as if they sensed the hunters nearby. Elephants were not just big, not just powerful, they were also highly intelligent and, some said, uncannily intuitive.

It was time. Henry unslung his gun; a Weatherby Mark V Deluxe, a piece of equipment designed to take a Weatherby Magnum .460 sporting cartridge, and, with minimum recoil, launch a 500-grain (32 g) bullet at a chronological velocity of 2,700ft/s from a 26 inch barrel. For 29 years the world's most powerful commercially available cartridge, now superseded only by the .577 T.Rex requiring a rifle so heavy as to be almost inoperable.

Henry was happy with his Magnum. It would be enough to penetrate the skull of the creature's 18″+ of cellular bone structure, the only shot that would kill on a full frontal charge. The rifle felt like a part of him. He stroked the barrel and stock lovingly, felt the power it had over him and the power it had over the world's most challenging prey; the bush elephant.

The herd were close by a shallow stream, barely visible in the high grass that surrounded them. The group of men slipped noiselessly into the water, guns held overhead, treading into mud until the water lapped around their chests. He could see the big bull he wanted and experienced a moment of intense pleasure. The tips of his fingers and toes tingled with an electric buzz. He closed his eyes for a second against the sun's white glare, breathed in deeply, smelled the elephant, sensed the heat shimmering off the tall grass. Despite the soaring temperature he felt cool and collected. The beast would soon be his, together with the accompanying kudos. Back at the camp his young lady would save all her attention for him. He'd have her tonight. Boy oh boy! Wouldn't he just.

He should wait until the bull turned, presenting a better target, but he was becoming impatient. Maybe go for an easier shot at the torso rather than the full on shot at a charging head. But no, he'd go for the head.

VANSITTART WAS BECOMING IMPATIENT; pacing the hotel room, the remains of a late breakfast of ham and eggs, bacon and sausage, french fries and hash browns congealing on the breakfast table, and on his umpteenth black coffee, he shouted into his mobile, "When the fuck're we going to have POC tied up, Cal? Been hammering away all day, and still short of 50 per!!"

"No problem Gil," came the calm voice of his broker Carleton Bass. "We're getting there. Give us a bit more time, the team are all working on it. A bit longer and we'll have Mr Wren all wrapped up in a steel mesh."

"Fucking pansy shouldn't be in business. We're in a man's game Cal. That girly Wren's, in the wrong game on the wrong pitch. Big game's what I'm after. Wren's not big game, he's a fucking rodent, a mouse; doesn't deserve the name CEO. We'll eat the fucker alive! Then we'll look for something a bit tastier. Yeah! Something we can really get our teeth into."

A knock at Wren's door. "Mrs Wren is here for you sir. Shall I show her in?" Mrs Collins, Wren's PA of 15 years looked in. A tall angular woman in her late forties, neither she nor Wren ever addressed each other with first names. "Thank you Mrs Collins, of course."

SHE WEARILY STRUGGLED to her feet for one last effort. She could hear the mewling of her weakening cub as she circled the gazelle. She moved in closer, closer, her belly grazing the ground. They were almost within her distance. One of the grazing gazelle looked up; looked around over its shoulder. None of the others seemed aware of anything untoward and the momentarily troubled member of the herd resumed grazing.

THE WATERS WERE SHALLOWER where Henry now stood, and he raised the rifle slowly, picking out the bull in his sights. Not the angle he wanted, but he couldn't wait any longer. He'd go for a heart/lung shot. Not what he'd planned, but he couldn't delay another moment. He had the animal's torso in the cross hairs of his sights and squeezed the trigger, easing it back, savouring the joy of the gun's explosive power. A whiff of cordite, smell of powder. Even the limited recoil set him back on his heels and he had to windmill his arms to prevent himself toppling backwards into the water. The shot went home, but missed the creature's vital organs, sending it into a trumpeting rage as it made off into the bush. "Hell's teeth, muttered one of the party. He'll go rogue now, no telling what he'll do where he'll show up."

WREN'S OFFICE was deadly quiet. His PA and several members of staff had come in and were sitting around, aimless. Mrs Collins, her navy two-piece suit, immaculate, sat demurely, her legs crossed, hands in her lap. She had a calming influence on all those around. "Can I get you anything Mr Wren?"

Wren turned from the screen he was studying and smiled at his imperturbable PA, "I'm fine for now thank you Mrs Collins." Susan sat next to her husband, who seemed increasingly distracted. The screens told a confused story with no-one entirely sure of what was going on. The only thing that seemed certain was that with Vansittart's final putsch to take over the company there'd be a lot of redundancies.

Vansittart was ecstatic. "Hey Cal, the motherfucker's on his knees. We're watching little Jenny die. Tell the truth, I never thought it'd be this easy."

———

SHE WAS as close as she could get now. One of the gazelle, the closest, had its back to her, upwind of her. As she accelerated out of the undergrowth the gazelle spotted her and flew fast to the left, but the lithe cat had anticipated the move as there was a termite mound to the right. In a moment she was up to her maximum speed, overhauling the gazelle as it twisted to left and right. Another few paces, the gazelle twisted again, maddeningly out of reach of the cheetah's range. She was going to fail, a final burst bringing her for the merest instant alongside, but too far behind to catch hold. Stretching herself to the limit she swept her front paw, that fifth claw, the thumb claw across the gazelle's hind leg. The creature faltered for a second, then recovered, changed direction, the wrong way and the cheetah pounced again, this time the thumb claw catching the front leg of the gazelle and bringing it down. She was on it in an instant, closing her jaw at its neck suffocating the creature. Her lungs were heaving as she stood over her kill. The cubs would eat today.

HENRY WAS FEELING both elated and yet the merest trifle apprehensive. It didn't do to be overconfident. It bred carelessness. Nerves were considered a good thing for a hunter of dangerous prey, as long as you held yours at the crucial moment. He'd hit the bull, weakened it, but the next move wasn't his, and the outcome would be unpredictable. One of the rangers had said to go back to camp. He'd repeated, a wounded bull could turn rogue, anything might be on the cards. Call off the hunt. But Henry was well aware of the power and accuracy of the Mauser, even if the ranger wasn't. He'd finish off the job today. An experienced hunter, whatever Henry's business shortcomings; here he was very much where he wanted to be. He breathed deeply, composed himself. His pulse slowed and he was icy calm. It wouldn't be long now.

It was less time than he thought. Henry barely had time to register the elephant's charge as it roared out of the bush and straight at him, its ears laid back flat. Thundering straight at Henry, raging in fury, dust clouding around its thundering legs and feet, the hunter was totally in his element, on familiar ground. He raised the gun calmly and coolly, all nerves dispelled and caught the elephant's skull between the cross hairs of the Mauser's sights and squeezed the trigger, with a no more than a split-second timing error, as the bull crashed into him, breaking his body, trampling him into the rock hard ground, a mess of crushed bones, torn tissue and blood.

"YIPPEEEE," Vansittart yelled. "You done it Call, you sweet bitch. You trampled little Jenny Wren into the dirt."

Wren looked ashen, small, beaten. His elbows on his desk, palms propping his chin, he gazed fixedly at a point over the heads of his employees, on the far wall of his office. He felt utterly weary. A fighter knows when he's beaten. His staff, those that had crept in to his office, looked desolate, some were clearly close to tears. Mrs Collins looked down at her hands, her face pale. Susan took her husband's hand, "I don't care, Jen," she said. "I don't care."

Wren said nothing, just stared at the phone on his desk as though it might suddenly start talking to him. Then it rang, its tone piercing as a gunshot aimed at Wren's head. He picked up the receiver slowly and put it to his ear. "Thanks Brian, I understand. I know, you've done all you possibly could. I am truly grateful. You know I couldn't have asked for a better broker. Come round later for a drink? Susan and I will expect you at 8.00? Fine."

"Ladies and gentlemen," Wren got to his feet and addressed those present. We've all been faced with a major challenge these last few hours and I have to tell you we're going to be facing much greater challenges in the future." There were murmurs among the staff. Frank and Edrich both looked lost, vacant. Nothing they'd done had been sufficient. Nothing could have foretold the events of the last hours.

Wren went on, leaning forward, hands on his desk, the feminine pitch of his voice soft and troubled. "Until now we, here at POC have operated as an independent making our own way, never seeking to amalgamate, take over or swallow up other vulnerable businesses, unless there was a joint advantage to be gained. It was never our style. We have today been faced with an unprecedented situation however, and I find I am obliged to apologise to all my staff for the ordeal you've been subjected to. Mr Vansittart of Vansittart Corporation has been engaged in a hostile purchase of our stock, using that very stock as collateral where he had insufficient funds to back his purchases. In short he has sought to purchase our company using our own stocks to assist in his purchase." Wren paused, unsure of whether the non-technical members of his team understood what he was explaining. "He's adopted that approach because he lacked the necessary immediate cash to behave in any other way. Interestingly, whilst we at POC are considerably smaller than Mr Vansittart's we have always maintained much greater cash balances simply because I've always been averse to unnecessary risk. I am aware that Mr Vansittart regards that manner of business as somewhat negative, somewhat lacking in his rather more brutal attitude."

"So where are we now Jen? Is it all over for us?" Edrich wanted to know.

"Is that really it?" said Frank.

Wren was frowning, shaking his head. "People," he said quietly. "I'm not making myself clear. I talked about extra challenges in the future simply because whilst Mr Vansittart was under the impression he was taking over our business, using his, I regret to say, distastefully high-risk tactics, my brokers and I with our resources, our greater cash floats and my judgement that we should get in first, have taken over Mr Vansittart's empire. I apologise, but it has been necessary for me to use the same shabby tactics as Mr Vansittart in order to stop him in his tracks. It is most unfortunate I realise, but it may be incumbent upon me to dispense with the services of Mr Vansittart himself in the immediate future. He really is too much of a risk taker. Not the sort of person that POC really wants to be associated with.

Chapter Five

KILLING ME SOFTLY

'He's dying, thank Christ, though he doesn't know it. Hasn't a clue.. Miserable shit that he is. Can't wait to have him gone.' The woman, in her fifties, with pockmarked skin, had mousy coloured hair in a pageboy cut, which abysmally failed in its presumed aim to make her jowled face look younger. The purple track-suit, which barely covered her more than ample frame, matched a complexion suggestive of a proclivity to high blood pressure. She gripped a smouldering half burned down cigarette between nicotine stained fingers that were tipped with chipped, black-rimed nails.

'You know Doreen, I always thought you two was set for life.' The older woman, probably in her late seventies, wore a flowered calf length dress and shiny pink satin headscarf tied in the 1940s peaked style over giant rollers.

'We had an okay marriage at the start I s'pose. Never what you'd call blinding, but okay. He was earning aw'right money running a betting shop. See Mave, maths had always been his thing. At fourteen, he could just about read, looked like he was a turning into a right idiot, but he was top of the top set in maths and computers at school. He was short and overweight, bullied by the others, bit like me, so we sort of got together.'

'A marriage made in heaven Dor.'

'Do me a favour. More like made in hell Mavis. I told you, I hate him.'

'Nah! Really? I mean, look at this home. Detached house overlooking Hampstead Heath. Roof garden. All mod cons. And those artificial flower arrangements you got all over the place. Totally beautiful. I never seen a kitchen like this one,' she said looking around at the display of black and white marble, strip lighting and expensive gadgetry. When I think of my damp Kilburn bedsit. Can't have got this lot from just working in a betting shop.'

'He didn't. But he was a gambler. All his life. That's how he made his money. Competition poker, in America. Cleaned up. Come home with his winnings. Two million dollars. All tax free. Online card-games, horses, dogs, football. He'd bet on who'd score what and when. Had a magic touch, and a computer for a brain. When we'd met, he'd had a wager with his one of his mates, one of the few,' she sniggered, 'had a bet he'd have me wed within the year.'

'And did he?'

'Have me wed?'

'Yeah.'

'Too right he did. Bought me jewellery, expensive holidays, a car; promised me the earth. Bought this house right after we got married.'

'Ooer,' said the other. Must have cost a bomb.'

'A bit. Spent a fortune on it. Worth a few million now, what with prices skyrocketing and so on. I mean, Hampstead.' She held her hands out expansively.

'Why'd he go on working then? I mean if he was so rich?'

'Bert's a lot richer now than he was. When we first moved in here, before he started gambling big time, he still needed a mortgage, and see, he needed to show regular earnings to get one. Anyway, he soon stopped the job. Didn't need it no more. Trouble is, once he stopped being employed he had to go on working at his gambling to keep up the life style. So he worked from home. Got under my feet. Drove me nuts I can tell you.' Doreen got up from the glass topped table pushing back the chrome and black kitchen chair, before walking over to where the gleaming conical kettle sat on the black marble work surface. Filling it from the ultra-modern mixer tap, she pressed the button in the handle for it to boil and sat down again with her friend Mavis.

The older woman glanced around the kitchen, and, taking a closer look, perceived signs of neglect she'd previously missed, or otherwise ignored. Scratches on the work surface, dust piles in corners of the room, a dent in the expensive kettle. There was dirty crockery ready to be placed in the dishwasher, but left unattended by the triple sink. Clothes, presumably ready for the washing machine, sat overlapping a plastic basket ready to be attended to. If one's first impression was luxury, the second was, shabby. It had the same tired look as the mistress of the house.

'What's wrong, Dor? Why ain't you happy?'

'He bores me, Mave.' Doreen contemplated the dog-end between her fingers, sighed and dropped it into a stray mug of tea dregs where it fizzed for a moment. 'Runs after me like a little dog. Men,' she exhaled. 'Every one of 'em like bleeding kids what wants attention all the time.'

'But you said he bought you gifts; told me he wanted to go on exotic holidays with you.'

'Yeah, well,' she said listlessly. 'I don't like cruises, get seasick. Don't like flying, all that turbulence. He took me to Paris once. Drove there. Eurostar. Got stuck in the bloody tunnel for an hour. When we get there, what do we find? I'll tell you what we find. It's nothing but frogs everywhere. Frogs to talk to. Frogs to eat. Bert likes all that stuff. But not me. Couldn't wait to get back home. Bloody garlic. I tell you, his breath. I said to him, you go on eating garlic love you can forget all about sex.'

'And did he?'

'What?'

'Give up garlic?

'Naw,' she guffawed. 'Thank gawd. All that huffin and puffin. Not for me darling. Never was.' Doreen got up and went over to the now whistling kettle. ''Nother cup Mave?'

'I won't say no Dor. Here,' she said, looking towards the kitchen doorway, 'What about Bert havin' a cup then?'

'He can wait,' shrugged Doreen.

'You really *don't* like him very much do you?'

'I told you, I hate him,' muttered Doreen, studying a bitten thumbnail which she proceeded to chew down a bit further. Then sighing, she poured them both fresh mugs of tea. 'And he knows it. Told him I wanted a divorce coupla years ago. But he wouldn't have it. Said he loved me. Said he'd got a bet with that same mate he'd stay married for at least 10 years. He said he was so sure we would, him and his mate put all their stake money with a lawyer to hold in escrow till the time was up. I mean, can you believe it? In escrow for God's sake. If he lost, the cash would go to his mate. But he wasn't going to lose, he said.'

'Do you know when the time is up then, Dor?'

'No, he wouldn't tell me. But I think I've worked it out, and it's any time soon. Then I'll get it.'

'Really? How are you going to get it, if he's all that clever?'

'Yeah, but he's not as clever as me. See, I told him he needed a hobby. Give his mind a rest from all that gambling, so he could get back to it refreshed. You know, batteries recharged and all that.'

'I don't see Bert as a hobbies man Doreen. What could he possibly be interested in?'

'Flower arranging, love. I taught him how to arrange flowers. Got him interested in colours and arrangements. Asked him to work out the odds of different flowers lasting for different lengths of time. He got really involved.'

'That was clever of you.'

'It was wasn't it,' said Doreen taking a sip from her steaming mug.

'Bit more sugar in mine, Dor?'

'Help yourself, Mave. It's by the kettle.' The older woman climbed off her chair and wandered over to add sugar to her tea from the black porcelain bowl on the worktop. 'While you're there Mave you might do me a favour and wash up those few bits. I'm absolutely out for the count you know.'

'Don't you want them in your machine Dor?'

'Nah. Better if they're done by hand. Mum always said they was better washed by hand. When you've done that, be a darling and put the clothes in the washing machine.'

Placing the crockery in soapy suds in the sink, Mavis stopped for a moment to survey the colourful arrangements. 'Did Bert do all of these then Dor?'

'That's right Mave. All artificial in the kitchen so's they wouldn't be affected by heat and steam when Bert was doing the cooking.'

'Bert did the cooking did he?'

'He did. All of it. I really couldn't be bothered. Not my thing.'

'Was there any real flowers he arranged then? Like, you know, fresh blooms?'

'Oh yeah,' said Doreen softly. 'But we kept those in his room didn't we.'

'In his room?'

'That's right, in his room.'

'Is he very ill then Dor? Shouldn't I take him up a cuppa or something now?'

'If you must then,' she sighed. 'But Mave, whatever you do, don't touch the flowers.'

Mavis returned after a few minutes, Doreen heard her clattering down the oak stairs in her old heavy lace-up shoes. 'He don't look so good Dor. I mean propped up in that bed. And he don't say much. Like it's a real effort to talk. And the sheets need changing something awful. Shouldn't you be…?

'No Mavis. I shouldn't.'

'Oh alright love. I was only asking. But…'

'Look Mavis, I run this household the way I want to. Me own mum and sister complained I was bossy. But believe me, when the chips was down after dad died, who'd they both look to? They looked to me. Trouble with Bert is he wouldn't take instructions. I said to him, Bert, if you want this place to run like clockwork you'll do as I say. But he was too bloody obstinate for his own good. Still insisted on doing his own thing. Man of the house, sort of. Thought he could best me eh? Made a mistake there didn't he. Hah! You gotta get up early to outdo Doreen Jobson.' Grasping her mug in both hands, Doreen looked into the surface of the tea as though it might tell her something. As if it might impart some hitherto hidden gem of knowledge.

'Why didn't you want me to touch the flowers Dor? They was lovely. Sort of purple violet. Bert had them arranged in vases and pots so they made the whole room bright. Though it looked like he could hardly see them. Like he was losing his sight an' that. Said you told him bright colours would help as his eyes was giving trouble. Like I said, his voice is really giving him gip an all. But why couldn't I touch them Dor?' Mavis had finished her mug of tea and sat fidgeting with a small black enamel pepper mill, one of a matching pair for salt and pepper, whilst staring intently at her friend.

'Because.' Doreen tapped the side of her nose.

'What's *because* mean?'

'It just means *because* Mave.'

'I was only asking,' Mavis sounded wounded.

'Look if you must know, I'm getting rid of him.'

'What? How're you doing that? I thought you said he was ill. Dying. I mean what's he dying of?'

'He is dying Mave. But the cancer's not that advanced yet.'

'Cancer? You didn't say nothing about him having cancer.'

'Could have another six to nine months there. No, right now he's dying of flowers.'

'Dying of flowers? Why whatever can you mean? How can he be dying of flowers?'

Ignoring the question, Doreen turned to face her friend and went on, 'The reason he don't talk to me no more is cos he can't hardly. Too blinkin' difficult. Sends me bleeding texts all day. As you noticed, he can't see neither, practically blind he is, but he's still placing bets. Can you believe it? Nothing bloody stops him. He's so bloody obsessed. Got that remote thing with the raised numbers on it so he can send texts to the bookies, and transfer monies around his bank account when he needs to. Least, that what he thinks,' she added cryptically. 'He can even time the texts, so if he's asleep when a race starts, it'll text through the bet for him anyway. He found an app what does it for him.'

Mavis's brow creased in perplexity, 'You've lost me love. Sending texts? Transferring money? Placing bets? I don't know what you're talking about.'

'Ok. Let me explain the whole thing.' Doreen leaned forward confidentially, her chin propped in her palms, elbows on the table and went on, 'Bert told me, years ago, that the only way you get to stay free in this life is when you eventually leave it. That's a joke isn't it? Die for liberation? Sounds like a bloody revolutionary if you ask me. On the other hand, he said, if you're planning on living a full free and happy existence, you can either scrape the bottom of the barrel, live like a tramp, or else you gets rich, aim for the top. No-one tells you what to do then when you got money to burn, he said. Except me,' she chuckled. 'He knew he could get rich through his gambling, so he said it would make him free. But I knew I'd need to keep him under control. And that's what I've done Mave. Couldn't have him doing too much of his own thing. Blimey, whatever next? He might be off with another woman. Some bit of fluff. That's if anyone else would have him.' Doreen sat back and closed her eyes, 'And we weren't gonna have that now were we,' she smiled.

'Dor,' said her friend shyly, 'What's that got to do with flowers?'

'Well now, I'll go into that,' said Doreen, leaning back and folding her arms across her voluminous bosom, 'First off, what Bert doesn't know is that I've got all his money.'

'No!' breathed the other. 'How'd you manage that?'

'Easy. When I convinced him he might be starting to lose it upstairs' she pointed to her temple, 'I hauled him off to the lawyers to sign up a lasting power of attorney.

'What's that do then Dor?'

'Hah!' shouted Doreen, 'Means I control the money. So quick as you like I transferred all his ready cash on the current and deposit accounts to me. I tell you Mave it was a bloody fortune he had there. Told him I was transferring a bit just for safekeeping. Left him a bit for his gambling.'

'Oh Dor. D'you think he knows you done it all?'

'Course he doesn't. Told you didn't I he's going gaga now, Mave. Totally.'

'But you said he was still gambling. How can he gamble if he's losing it? Don't sound to me like he's losing anything,' she said speculatively.

'He needs me Mave. He can't look after hisself. Before I started with the flowers Doc told him he had pancreatic cancer, give him 12 to18 months. Bert said to me that'd take him up to the ten years we been married and he'd get his winnings. I'm mean, bleeding hell, he's dying and he still wants to win a bet? He told me he's not worried about dying. So I thought I might hurry things along a bit. Those flowers you like so much Mave, they're called monkshood, or devil's helmet. They're blinking lethal to the touch. And all the while he's been able to he's been arranging 'em.' Doreen rocked back on her chair and cackled like a hyena, displaying worn silver capped pre-molars. 'And he don't know none of it. Fancy, he's been killing hisself for months with the flowers, and in between times winning lots'a money for me to spend when he's gone.' Doreen held her sides hooting till the tears ran down her face. 'I puts on rubber gloves, takes him the flowers and a vase, and he puts them in, far as he can still see them. Tells me they smell lovely. Hah!' she exploded again. 'Says his fingers is numb. I'll say they're numb.'

'Oh Dor; should you be doing all that? I mean, Bert's not a bad bloke. After all, killing him?'

'He's a bloody pain the rear end Mavis. And I've got him where I want him. He's not bettered me. No-one does. He'll be gone shortly, then I'm free. You hear? Free and rich and alive Mavis, to do what I want with my life.'

'Yes Dor. Of course,' said Mavis quietly. 'You probly won't want to see me no more in my little flat.'

'Don't be daft Mave. Course I will. Bit damp, but cosy. Nothing's gonna change darling,' Doreen shuddered, despite herself at the thought of the place. There was fungus on the ceiling and evidence of rodent infestation in the kitchen, the bathroom was unspeakable and now come to think of it, her friend's sour perspiration featured more strongly on its home ground than elsewhere. All thoughts she quickly banished from her mind; she always kept her rare visits there short anyway.

The mobile in Doreen Jobson's tracksuit pocket bleeped and she looked down at it in irritation. 'What's he want now?' she muttered bringing up the screen. Then she smiled grimly, feeling an unaccustomed thrill of anticipation. Nearing the end now. She could sense it. Soon be free. Free of him for all time. Reaching into a pocket of the tracksuit she extracted a cigarette from the pack and flamed the tip with her lighter. This was going to be good, so, time to reward herself with a smoke, she thought, inhaling satisfyingly before starting to read out loud, 'Here listen to this Mave. It's from him upstairs. What a laugh this'll be.'

"Darlingest Dory, I know I've been a nuisance these last few months, but when the doctor said I had a year or so to go I really wanted to be as little trouble as possible for you, knowing how hard you've tried to make my life bearable. So glad you changed your mind about the divorce. I'd have been lorst without you; you manage the house so much better than I ever could. You was always so good me, an that. Course, you remembered I wasn't scared of dying, and you must

know how grateful I am to you for helping things along without saying nothing about that devil's helmet you give me. It's been a real blessing. Speeded up the process and that. No fuss. Sort of killing me softly, like that song innit. You might say, just what the doctor ordered. Ha ha.

Then I knowed you might get confused about the money, and obviously you were, cos all that cash kept going into your accounts from out of mine. But, no matter, I was able to transfer it all back. This little clicker's been really handy as my sight's got worse. Practically blind now. Can't see to do nothing properly no more.

But now I really need to apologise to you cos of what I never said; I hit a streak of bad luck after the cancer diagnosis last year and started losing and kept on losing, till now there's nothing left. Not a bean. I even re-mortgaged the house while I was still able to. Also, I won that bet six months ago, about keeping wed for 10 years, and lorst all that money as well.

Then I thought, I can't be a burden to my Dory no more, she's done so much for me, so I been eating the flowers you left by the bedside, them devil's helmet, for the last hour or so and I think I'm going now. I set the timer so this text would reach you after I'd be gone. I'm not afraid. And I know you'll manage okay without me when the bank sells the house to redeem the mortgage. Maybe put up with your friend Mavis for a bit. I'm sure she'll have you. You said she had a lovely little flat in Kilburn.

At least we'll both be free now. It's what you wanted I know.

Sorry about the money.

Your own,

Bert. Xx

Chapter Six

IN HIS OWN IMAGE

*A*rchie Clement scalped his first Yankee when he was just seventeen years of age. Egged on by his fellow bushwackers the baby-faced rebel engaged in the final stage of what sociologist Lonnie Athens has described as, 'the violentization' of man. Archie had never felt better. The incident had given him a sense of peace and well-being that he would have found impossible to describe.

Standing barely five feet tall. Clement would shortly become a giant among his peers, all members of William T (Bloody Bill) Andersen's gang of Missouri terrorists. This, his first victim, a suspected Union man and abolitionist had pleaded on his knees for the lives of his wife and two little girls, but Clement, smiling, had casually shot them anyway. Again, the feeling was indescribable. Then, as their father had lain prone, an earlier bullet having entered his left lung. Clement had taken his jagged edged Bowie knife and slit open the man's stomach from just above the pubic bone to the base of his rib cage. Seeing his abdomen yawn wide, displaying viscera heaving like a barrel of snakes, the helpless individual had screamed in agony and fear. Quite unconcerned, Clement had turned the man onto his front, and then with the deliberation of a farmer branding a heifer, bent a knee into the prisoner's back, a hank of his hair hauled up in one hand, the Bowie knife in the other. Then he'd traced fine lines of blood with the point of the blade across the back of the man's neck, down the sides of his head and behind the ears, and then finally across the hairline at the front of his forehead.

The victim had guessed what was coming, and begged Clement again for his life; and if not that, then at least to end it quickly. Young Archie had paused for a moment in his endeavours, as though thinking perhaps he'd done enough for one day. Dozens had been slaughtered by the gang over the last few hours in an orgy of destruction. The man would not survive anyway. Let him bleed to death like the son of a bitch he was. Maybe put a lead ball into his head. A quick kill, like the man's family had enjoyed. Something to ponder.

William Andersen's band of border ruffians, which included the notorious Frank and Jesse James, had been formed in the latter years of the American Civil War. Bloody Bill was a disillusioned man of twenty-five whose father had been killed in the Kansas area. Then, the Kansas City prison collapse had killed one of his sisters and injured the other two, leaving Bill a man raging for revenge. (man of twenty-five who's father had been killed in the Kansas Territory; one of his sisters had died in the Kansas City prison collapse, and two others had been injured.) Starting out as a simple bandit,(Delete: a man bent on revenge), he had graduated to leading his own group of followers in early 1864. Killing and looting their way across the counties of Chariton, Randolph, Monroe, Howard and Boone, they were once heard to boast (to one sobbing woman,) "We would shoot Jesus Christ or God Almighty if he ran from us."

Clement was still thinking what he should do. Compassion wasn't his strong point. But still, the man had shown some courage, begging for his family before himself. Indeed, offering himself in their stead. And, there again, there were no guarantees he was a Union man after all. A good soldier knows when to show mercy to his prisoner. Clement breathed deeply, savouring the moment. Should he favour the man with a quick kill? Perhaps after all he might…

The shriek sounded like an explosion to all those around as Clement scalped the man, tearing out the fist of hair, with a sound like ripping cloth. Usually victims were dead before they were subjected to this form of treatment. But Archie Clement had decided after all to bring an element of innovation to his particular brand of retribution against this Northern scum.

But Archie wasn't all work; the boy had a sense of humour, joining in the laughter when other gang members joshed him affectionately about his chipped front teeth, broken in a fall from a horse, or gave him stick over his rank smelling breath. He chewed tobacco constantly, ate little and drank only whiskey, with the result that his dry mouth gave off an aroma of rancid milk, nicotine and booze. The stench was truly appalling, but Clement took it as part of his autograph, and revelled in it.

The group rode on. Clement, who's frequent advice had hitherto been noted by Bloody Bill, but seldom taken up, would now be followed more often. The boy was a fully paid up member and had a lot to offer.

The outlaw, Jesse James was particularly impressed with the gang's young protégé, describing Clement as, "one of the noblest boys, and the most promising military boy, of this age." Indeed James was delighted in early May 1865 to assist two others of the gang in holding down a fighting militiaman while Clement, with a surgeon's skill, cut his throat and scalped him.

In the same month, Clement, who'd now been full rein, organised raids, first in the village of Holden and later the town of Kingsville, Johnson County. At 2 am they'd roared through the village streets, shooting down men and boys as they scrambled from their beds, looting shops and burning homes. Then as dawn approached, the town of Kingsville was treated to the benefit of the gang's unique attention. Bloody corpses littered the main street and smoking wreckage (smouldering ruins) completed the clan's signature. A Confederate soldier in the vicinity stated that he'd seen Clement at the head of some seventy men, describing him as, "Bill Anderson's scalper and head devil." When news of the comment reached Archie Clement, he'd whooped with delight. A young man needed respect and recognition of his abilities. He was making his way and making his mark. He couldn't have been happier.

The following year, in February 1866, Clement was involved in the robbery at the Clay County Savings Association in the town of Liberty. This would be an ambitious project by any man's standards, and Archie was nervous before the heist. For once, more than a little unsure of himself. Not certain if he could pull it off. He'd planned the whole thing with his usual meticulous care, but still, he was nagged by doubts. Had he picked the right day? Would the bank have the hoped for reserves in their safe? Had he anticipated the number of security men they'd need to deal with? Too many unknowns for the boy to handle. Before the start, his throat had been tight with nerves. His palms damp with apprehension. He crossed himself and sallied forth. Jesus would be with him.

In the event, his gang had been involved in a major shoot-out. Things started to look bad, very bad. Bullets ripped through Clement's buckskin cleaving furrows of blood in his shoulders and thighs, but leaving him otherwise intact, for the moment. Realising he'd badly underestimated the opposition he might come up against, Clement had at first been weak with terror. But of what? Death? No. Archie Clement was terrified of failure. Of appearing diminished in the eyes of his fellows. Otherwise, the whole venture had left him exhilarated. As a rain of lead shot had avalanched through the gang, Archie Clement had laughed aloud. And in the end he'd survived, giving thanks to his Maker for bringing him through.

The haul was in excess of $58,000. Surprisingly, only one man died as the gang made their getaway. But Archie Clement had come through. It was then that he realised, beyond any doubt, he led a charmed life. Nothing could touch him. Nothing ever would. God was on his side. The posses that chased them finally lost the trail at Sibley, a favoured crossing point of the bushwackers on the Missouri river.

That night, as the Clement group made camp, the young man surveyed the men around him with a sense of satisfaction. They'd cleared a lot of money in the operation, and they'd had a lot of fun. Next time, maybe, there'd be the chance to put away a few more of the town's good citizens. Blood needed to be spilt if people were to remember to take caution when dealing with Clement and his mentor, Bloody Bill Anderson. The important thing was, that with Bill and Archie's stewardship, the gang were strong, clever and way ahead of the law when it came to setting up operations. There was little chance they'd be apprehended. Their pursuers knew what awaited them if ever they happened to catch up with Archie.

THOMAS C FLETCHER had been voted Governor of Missouri in the 1864 elections. Fletcher had shown himself to be a man of immense courage and resourcefulness when, as a brigadier general in the army of Tennessee, he'd seen action during the Civil War. A Radical and committed abolitionist, he was not a man to be trifled with. Fletcher pledged himself and the people of the state of Missouri to rid themselves of the scourge of banditry.

Tossing out Conservative officeholders at every level, when a number of hardliners in Lafayette County refused to go, Fletcher enlisted a company of militia to literally drag them from office, two of them being imprisoned, with some degree of irony, in Lexington's old slave jail. (incarcerated, with somewhat poetic justice, in the old slave jail in Lexington). Clearly, the man meant business. During the rest of 1864 and the following year, Fletcher organised what was to be his eventual planned attack on the bushwacker threat in general, and Archie Clement in particular. One way or another, the Clement menace would be addressed.

Fletcher was also a patient man, but the responsibilities of office together with difficulties in organising a response to the renegades meant that it was December 1866 before he was able to act. In late November, Archie Clement, Dave Pool and a gang of some hundred or so outlaws (desperados) had ridden through the town of Lexington, terrorising its citizens. Matters were coming to a head.

Fletcher had additionally organised a detachment of militia, which on December 2nd were heading for Lexington. He'd also ordered the recruitment of further volunteers. (Fletcher, meanwhile had organised a platoon of militia, which on December 2nd were heading for Lexington, and he'd additionally issued calls for further volunteers). The thirty-seven militiamen who arrived that day were headed by a tall, broad shouldered man called Bacon Montgomery.

Archie Clement wasn't in the least worried; he knew he had the town of Lexington under his thumb. He smiled inwardly when he and twenty-six rebels rode into town on the morning of 13th December ostensibly to form a militia company in accordance with Fletcher's order. Cynically joining forces with those seeking to obliterate them would be an act of supreme arrogance. Needless to say, it appealed to Clement's sense of irony. He'd be a fully accredited militiaman, charged with the task of rooting out bandits, like himself.

Bacon Montgomery knew damn well what was happening, but, behaving with calm aplomb, allowed the guerrillas to enlist, before he ordered them to leave town.

Clement, ignoring the edict, decided to stay, and took himself to the bar of the old City Hotel where he met a friend for a drink.

Learning of this heaven sent opportunity, Montgomery now instructed (ordered) three of his men, J.M.Turley, George Moses and Tom Tebbs to arrest Clement in the hotel bar. Then, deciding to take absolutely no chances, sent one, Sergeant Joe Wood after the other three. Wood was known to be an uncompromisingly aggressive individual.

Clement fingered the Bowie knife at his waist, making sure it was secure. The touch of the bone handle against his palm gave him a slight adrenalin rush. The whiskey was warming to the stomach; just what a man needed when he'd now enlisted in the militia to help capture desperate renegades. The two pistols in his belt were fully loaded. Clement was as handy with those as he was with the knife. Clement's colleague had noticed nothing. But then few men had Clement's heightened sense of awareness. Few men had his animal feel for lurking danger. He took in everything around him, his eyes restlessly darting this way and that. It's what had kept him alive this long. With God's grace, it would keep him alive for a whole lot longer.

Clement immediately spotted the three men, Turley, Moses and Tebbs, when they entered the bar. They looked as though they might want to strike up a conversation with him. Why not? Clement thought. The three ordered drinks and then edged towards the young man. Clement had quickly recognised them for what they were, and, with a frisson of pleasure in his chest, realised he was in for a bit of amusement. He'd take out the tall one first, then deal with the other pair. Two dark haired, one fair. Three smart scalps to add to his saddle. His mouth watered slightly, his eyes narrowed and he waited.

Then, without warning, Wood crashed (burst) in, shouting, "Surrender," and all hell broke loose.

Clement jumped out of his chair, drawing his two revolvers as his friend made a dash for the stairs. Moses fired, felling Clement's friend with a bullet in the leg. Clement, grinning to himself, chased into an (a side) office where, in the next instant, a searing flash of pain burned into his chest; a shot from Moses had found its mark. Bursting (Crashing) out of the hotel, Clement found his horse and, hauling himself into the saddle, made to escape down the street while firing back at his pursuers.

It was clear to Clement that he had the advantage, despite the wound. He'd make his getaway and hole up somewhere. Get some medical attention. Plenty of families in the area sympathetic to rebels. Then when he was patched up he'd meet with the rest of the boys and get back to Lexington to teach those bastards a lesson they'd not forget.

He spurred his horse on through the centre of town making a gain on his pursuers and was oblivious to the thunder (roar) of gunfire that greeted him as he passed the courthouse where Bacon Montgomery had thoughtfully placed the rest of his militiamen. His horse pulled up. And Clement was aware of burning sensations in his arms and legs and body as he was buffeted by a hail of bullets. He could taste dust, and realised he'd fallen into the dirt. Notwithstanding his injuries, he knew he'd give those sons of bitches a run. His arms were weakening, and in order to cock his pistol, he needed to pull at the hammer with his broken front teeth. But he simply couldn't make the connection with the chipped stumps. Still, he'd have their bloody scalps. Just wait. He'd have them all, the scum.

Archie didn't know how long he was out, but when he came to, he found himself lying bare chested on a grassy hillock overlooking Lexington. It was a glorious cloudless day and the sun beat down on his body. He was mended and feeling great. Human again. Nothing in the world like that feeling. Archie Clement, invincible. The man with a charmed life.

Then he got to thinking back. Try as he might he couldn't remember how he'd made his escape. One of the boys must have come back for him. That was it; maybe Bill himself. Or perhaps it was Frank or Jesse. You could always rely on the James boys. Whatever, Archie Clement had survived and lived to fight another day. Archie Clement always survived. Hadn't he always said those Republican filth would never take him alive? He smiled and breathed in deeply the fresh spring air. Spring? It must be months since... He was still puzzled.

Over to his right gazing down at the town, hands casually on his hips, was a guy he'd not spotted before. Short, powerfully built. So that was who... Dave Pool? No. Dave had been wounded too. Who the hell?

Then the man turned around and looked at Archie. "You're awake." He smiled easily and came trotting over to Clement. Archie noticed the man was quite young, about his own age. He carried a couple of pistols in his belt and a Bowie knife, like Archie's own armoury, at his waist.

The man reached forward as though intending to shake hands with Archie, and Archie in turn lifted his hand in response, only to find the other look backward over his shoulder before whipping out his own Bowie. He'd seen or heard someone coming up behind him and was clearly on his guard, every bit as sharp as Archie.

Clement, straining to look over the other's shoulder to find what it was that had disturbed him, was shocked to feel the point of the Bowie burrow deep into his groin, where it seemed to pause for an instant, before ripping wide his stomach as far as the breast bone. He looked down stupefied, saw his guts yawn red and wide; watched as his viscera heaved like a mess of knotted worms. "What the fuck?" He snarled.

The man stank of something unidentifiable, but Archie had little time to contemplate his assailant's fragrance, for the man had swiftly rolled Clement on to his front.

Archie could feel grass, dust, pebbles, grit lodging in the open cavity of his stomach and it made him feel sick. All those months of healing, now he'd have to go through it all...

A knee pressed into Clement's back and a strong hand grasped a hank of his hair. If Archie hadn't known what was going to happen before, he knew now, beyond any shadow of a doubt. And the thought filled him with dread. For the first time in his life he felt real fear. A metallic taste flooded his mouth, and the hammering in his chest and neck and ears only served to emphasise his terror. A trickle of sweat ran down the back of his neck. This wasn't going to be a quick death.

Fighting to control his galloping panic. Clement ground his teeth, then said as calmly as he could, "Look, Mister, maybe we can talk this thing over."

"What did you have in mind?" said the other, as he traced the point of the Bowie across the back of Clement's neck.

"Why are you doing this?"

"Tell the truth, I hadn't thought about it too much."

"Are you a Yankee?"

"Can't say I am," he replied, drawing a bead of blood with the tip of the knife at the sides of Clement's head and behind his ears.

"For God's sake, man, stop it."

"For whose sake?" the man chuckled. "What do you know about God?"

"Listen, I'm a regular church going Baptist. My mamma and my papa...

"Okay, son. Maybe I'll give it some thought."

Clement felt the pressure on his scalp relax for a moment, and he breathed tentatively, a sigh of relief. It's going to be all right he decided. Hearing a sound like ripping cloth, Clement's jaws tore at the air in a scream so strangled the strain burst blood vessels in his throat and he spat blood. He fell forward and sideways, seeing the man holding the macabre trophy for Clement to see. That rancid stink again. Then it all went black.

When Archie regained consciousness he was lying, his shirt open, on his back near to some woodland. Trees nearby showed their autumn colours, and the sun shone through patchy clouds. He was well again. Mended, as before. But how? And where?

Seated near to him was a young man, about his own age. Archie frowned, totally confused.

"You're awake then," the young man turned towards Clement, he smiled easily. Getting to his feet, he approached Clement, who looked up at him fearfully. As the other slid the Bowie from his belt Archie knew what was going to happen and he heaved up a great pipe of vomit in his fear. The slicing open, then the cutting and ripping of Archie's scalp had him shrieking in agony.

When he opened his eyes and looked down at his body, healed and mended as before, he knew no sense of relief. Only a fear so great he doubted he could survive it. His body was wracked, his hands perspired, he was running rivulets of sweat. It felt as though his heart must give out of its own accord.

And there was the young man, once again, the Bowie in his hands. His breath stank familiar, a mixture of rank milk, nicotine and whiskey. He leaned down and with the blade, opened up a chasm in Clement's stomach. As Archie screamed again, tearing his throat to shreds, he looked up at his tormentor, into eyes he recognised only too well. The other young man was smiling. An avuncular smile, revealing a set of broken front teeth.

"I know you," choked Clement, as the two men's eyes met.

"1 should think you probably do," replied the young man.

"It's you, isn't it," he cried. "I know you! My God! I know you! My God! It is thee."

Chapter Seven

MRS ROSENFELD'S GHOST

The room was in deep shadow, its sole illumination a fragmented circle of light cast by the thin beam of a table lamp. Alan Strong sat at his desk and gazed up at the ceiling. A big man, and powerful personality, he did not scare easily. If you'd asked him a few years ago whether he believed in ghosts he'd have laughed in your face. Yet now his heartbeat quickened until his chest hurt. His hair prickled at the back of his neck and a belt of icy cold damp encircled his waist, climbing up his spine and sides until he felt its chill penetrate to the very marrow of his bones.

But the baby was fast asleep.

He waited quietly, knowing it was going to start again, and knowing there was nothing he could do about it. Any moment; he held his breath and waited. The seconds ticked by. Now he could feel it all around him, growing, building until the room was full of it; its presence clinging to him with octopus tentacles. The area became saturated with the smell of musk, so strong it made his eyes smart and his nose quiver as though he might suddenly sneeze.

The baby slept on.

Still he remained unmoving, breathing quietly, expectantly.

Then at last he heard what he'd been anticipating. Moving into focus overhead. It was coming from the loft, the gentle tap tap tapping of a stick, and the hesitant tread of an elderly person creeping cautiously on the roof beams on the floor above him. Except that there were no floorboards in the loft, only ancient rafters, each set more than a foot apart from one another. He knew now, beyond any doubt, it was with him for good, he could never escape it. It would hound him until his death. It would quicken his death.

But the baby remained undisturbed.

He'd been just sixteen when things had started to change.

BOOM, BOOM, BOOM, BOOM. The strains of one rock'n'roll record after another reverberated throughout the magnificent house. The floorboards juddered and walls trembled in time to the music.

Sixteen year old Alan Strong spread his long legs, eased back on the armchair in his bedroom and smiled to himself as he felt the adrenalin flow tingling in his hands and feet. This was more like it. Saturday morning, best time of the week. No hurrying to school, no teachers complaining about his continual insubordination and no dewy eyed Jenny Morgan mooning after him. Just forget all about life's problems and lose yourself in the music. Wonderful. The beat was compelling, insistent, reflecting his vision of himself. Young and forceful with limitless opportunities ahead. He stretched his arms and flexed his muscles, running his fingers though his thick black hair. Then, climbing out of the chair, he did a shuffling dance around the room. He felt good. Life was waiting for him to grab it, and that was what he intended to do. Success beckoned. Follow in Dad's footsteps in the family firm. He couldn't lose.

Alan's mother, Deidre, a prim looking woman in her early forties, was becoming familiar with her teenage son's taste in this `new' type of music. But then she knew she was merely putting a brave face on things. Though she was loath to admit it to herself, in her heart she was increasingly worried by the changes she was witnessing in her husband. He was ageing as she looked at him. So far though, she was aware, her husband had not elected to confide in her.

Mr Strong, a greying, rangy, intense man increasingly preoccupied with fast becoming insurmountable business problems, showed little interest in his son's music. He was a man looking for answers. But until now he'd chosen to remain silent about what it was that was worrying him. He wouldn't be remaining silent for very much longer.

That left Graham, Alan's eleven year old brother, who viewed the world with juvenile indulgence, concentrating his energies mainly on baiting next door's cat.

The summer of 1959 had been an idyll of sunshine, and the thundering sound of drums and amplified guitars, with no hint of the business reversals that Mr Strong would suffer as the year drew to a close. Life was about to become transformed for them all, irrevocably.

His face was distorted with worry, and he scratched the back of his head distractedly, "Don't breathe a word to the boys till after Christmas," Mr Strong counselled his wife, "Seems a pity to spoil it for them. But, I'm afraid, things are going to have to change for us." He sighed. "It'll be no picnic."

Mrs. Strong had never seen her husband so strained, but she too was worried, in need of some reassurance. She put an arm about his shoulders and nodded sadly, "What about our lovely home, Henry? Will we be able to keep it with all that money you say the business owes? And if we can't, wherever shall we live?"

Mr. Strong breathed deeply. "Thankfully house prices have shifted up since we moved from Kilburn to Hampstead," Taking his wife's hand in his own, he smiled calmly at her. "We should be able to stay in this area, my dear, though no longer in a detached house, I'm afraid. We'll cope, just about; though nothing is going to be what we've been used to up to now."

"And the debts?" She still felt worried. "What about all the money we owe?"

"Not us, Deidre. The business. I'm going to have to reorganise the company, cut back everywhere, pay off the creditors as best I can, and get us a small flat." He closed his eyes as he considered the future. "The lads will be disappointed of course. You'll tell them, my dear; when the time is right, you're better at that sort of thing."

Mrs. Strong's manner with her sons was brisk, hiding the tide of apprehension that threatened to overwhelm her. "There's nothing for it boys; Daddy has said we're moving to an apartment in one of those nice mansion blocks." She tried hard to smile through her sadness and fear. "There'll be a bit less space, I'm afraid, but nothing else should change. You'll both be able stay at Kynaston School." It would be little consolation for them both, and she knew it.

Mrs. Strong reflected for a moment, "Oh! There *is* one thing. The noise. You'll have to keep the volume of that record player down. I'm sorry Alan," she said, her voice rising in irritated response to her older son's growls of protest, "There's no `Oh! Mum' about it. There'll be other people to consider now, so that's how it's going to have to be."

OAK TREE MANSIONS, in St. John's Wood, was a forbidding, red brick Edwardian building in a narrow and sullen looking street. Its dark and cheerless interior was characterised by patched, brown linoleum flooring and a tiny lift with immovable expanding gates. The smell, on entering the damp block, was sour and musty. The atmosphere, chill. Its inhabitants, equally joyless, comprised it seemed, mainly octogenarians who viewed the newcomers with overt suspicion. The building seemed like a mute retribution to Mr. Strong's business downfall. It was all desperately depressing.

Alan felt the gloom of the place enfold him like a black cloud. What a change! How could they have come down to this? "What a dump, Mum," he complained. "I'm going to hate it here. Hope I never get into the same cash bind as dad." Then he smiled, "I s'pose there's always Elvis to brighten things up."

"Now Alan," said his mother, with a frown, "remember what I said about keeping the noise down. We're not in a detached house anymore. We've got to remember the neighbours in the block. Absolutely no ifs and buts about it."

Their newly decorated three-bedroom apartment itself was acceptable enough. However, living in a flat was going to require the family to make adjustments that Alan particularly would find it hard, if not impossible to reconcile themselves with.

The family had been installed in the apartment no more than a week, when they first met Mrs Rosenfeld. Alan was bored, had been since they'd arrived. The flat was always cold, the central heating wholly inadequate. The hell! He'd made desultory efforts to turn down the record player from time to time, but with little discernible effect. Why bother when what the neighbours thought was really of no consequence to him. They'd simply have to get used to it.

The front bell rang that evening at about eight, just as the family were preparing to eat. Now, at his father's insistence, Alan grudgingly turned off the roaring gramophone, and the walls and floor instantly stopped shuddering to the thumping beat.

Accompanied by his wife and two curious sons in tow, Mr Strong went to the door. The four of them were confronted by a stocky lady in her late sixties. Her white hair was tied back in a bun, which she primped nervously with one hand. She wore a grey shawl about her round shoulders and leaned heavily on a cane walking stick. Peering over tortoise shell pince-nez she addressed the family in a guttural, Central European accent.

"I am Mrs Rosenfeld from ze flet below. Such a noise! Such a noise! You could please make qvuieter. I have to see patients in ze day. In ze evening I must rest. I need peace."

Alan was frankly intrigued by their neighbour. Couldn't make her out. Who on earth, he wondered, did that dumpy old lady imagine she was going to attract with that overpowering perfume she wore?

"I'm sorry you've been disturbed Mrs Rosenfeld," apologised Mrs Strong, a friendly hand on her elderly neighbour's shoulder. "I'll see to it my son keeps the music down. While you're here, can we offer you something? A drink perhaps? Or a cup of tea?"

"Senk you no. For me it is late, and I am tired".

The old lady, fluttered her eyelashes like a shy child and Alan thought he'd noticed something else quite strange about her; she appeared to have one blue eye and one brown. Stranger and stranger, he thought. She gave the family an odd, yet distinctive, lopsided sort of grin and primped her bun again. Then she left her calling card and, as she departed, shaking her head, her walking stick tapping on the linoleum floor, they heard her muttering under her breath,

"Music? Zey call zis music? Gott in Himmel! GOTT...IN...HIMMEL!"

The card read, 'Mrs Rosenfeld, Child Psychologist,' and gave the address of the flat directly below the Strongs', and her telephone number.

"She certainly seems perplexed by you two, doesn't she?" said mother, pensively.

"Anyway boys; I've said it before and I'll say it again, from now on, keep the clamour down. Is that understood?"

The lads nodded in unison. Then Alan added, "Funny how she kept fidgeting with her hair and fluttering her eyes. And that perfume! What a smell." He paused, "And how about that weird smile, Mum?"

OVER THE ENSUING months and years that witnessed Mrs Rosenfeld's seemingly endless litany of complaints, the brothers repeatedly lowered the sound levels of the gramophone, only to let it creep back up again until the old lady was forced to approach their front door, or write letters of complaint. Mr and Mrs Strong did their best to remonstrate with their sons, but had, in the days of the old house, become so accustomed to the cacophony, that they appeared to be unaware themselves of what constituted an acceptable volume.

For herself, Mrs Rosenfeld found the noise intolerable. A gentle and cultured woman with a love of classical music, she was seldom able to listen to her own choice of records because she was simply unable to hear them over the din from the floor above. She had chosen to live in Oak Tree Mansions specifically because it appeared to be a quiet old-fashioned block. Now this rude shattering of her tranquillity left her saddened and bemused. For all of her professional skills, she could think of no way to deal with the arrogant young man upstairs. She'd always loved children, always found that patience and a kind word produced wonders. But nothing seemed to work with Master Strong who treated her with contemptuous disdain. She could feel her health and life's force diminish daily under the continuous bombardment of sound. But she was powerless to do anything about it.

Alan, who had continued to rely on the heavy beat music to help him unwind after long hours of studying at school, became ever more enraged by Mrs Rosenfeld's protests. He couldn't imagine life without rock'n'roll. It was a like drug to him. A balm. Why couldn't she understand that and leave him alone. The woman was clearly a troublemaker, complaining for its own sake. He now tended to refer to her, dismissively, as 'Old Rosy,' or 'Rosyfeld.' "No-one else ever complains," he muttered furiously to his mother.

"No-one else lives directly below us darling," she replied in a weak attempt to reign in her son.

"Just try to accommodate her, please. She is very old now." But in her heart she knew that was never going to happen, nor could she have foreseen the consequences of her son's intransigence.

Alan matured into a, handsome young man, with a winning smile and a promising legal career ahead of him. His future now determined, Alan had become ever more confident and assured. Henrietta, whom he married six months before his solicitor's finals were due, was dark haired and petite, with somewhat fragile health; a recently diagnosed a heart murmur, it seemed. They'd intended to wait; but there was the chance to rent a refurbished flat, that Henrietta had discovered, in a small, church like, Victorian block in Hampstead. Not the most beautiful of buildings, but still an opportunity not to be missed. Alan had his doubts about the old house. Nothing he could specify. Just something that troubled him. He'd taken a two year sabbatical after University, and the couple now felt that after a five year courtship - they'd met on campus when she was reading Sociology - they'd waited long enough to be together.

Mrs Rosenfeld had been sent an invitation to the wedding out of courtesy. Or perhaps conscience. But she'd died suddenly, the family were informed, some time before the ceremony.

Alan had largely forgotten about her, with the odd exception of those nights when he could have sworn he could smell the distinctive musk of her perfume as he dropped off to sleep. Also, he'd dreamt of her once or twice. Seen the white hair done in a bun and that odd smile of hers behind his eyelids. But each time, the dream had turned sour as Alan had witnessed the old lady's smile become a sabre toothed snarl. He dismissed it all as of no consequence, even when, on one occasion he'd woken in a cold sweat.

The final years of Mrs Rosenfeld's life had not been serene, despite the Strongs' intermittent attempts to allow for her apparent eccentricities. In the last four or five years they'd hardly seen her at all. She seemed to have retired from practice;

certainly there were no more unsettled children accompanied by anxious parents beating a path to her door. And the complaints had finally ceased. Alan had had no time for the old lady anyway, calling her, "A damn nuisance from a bygone age."

"There's no doubt about it," Alan had announced gleefully to his brother one day, a couple of years earlier, as a fifteen minute Ginger Baker drum solo faded, "She likes the music. Old Rosy, has finally become a fan. We never get a peep out of her any more. Maybe I should try to sell her my old Beatles collection." And he'd laughed uproariously at his own joke.

"Come off it," Graham had remonstrated, "You can push your luck too far, Alan, even with that old biddy."

The young couple planned to move into the one-bedroom conversion, immediately after the honeymoon. Alan, now employed by a West End firm of solicitors, proposed to concentrate on studying for his finals. He'd work like mad for the next six months with the object of securing a first time pass. Henrietta, would focus on her career as an administrator in the social service department of the local council. Then with their joint earnings they could save for the deposit on a place of their own.

Alan's doubts about the house surfaced again just before the couple moved in. The odd creaks and groans of doors and floorboards, particularly when he was alone in the house. The feeling that someone was watching him from over his shoulder.

The high ceilinged Victorian building was divided into five self-contained units, with all but one, occupied by young marrieds. The sole empty flat that remained was situated directly over the Strongs', the others ranging to the rear and sides of the odd shaped building. It meant that Alan and Henrietta would hear no one from the other apartments and Alan would have the quiet necessary to concentrate on his studies. At least until someone moved in to the flat above.

The couple were tired the first night in their own home after the honeymoon and turned in early. Safe in her husband's arms,

Henrietta fell asleep as soon as her head touched the pillow. Alan cuddled up to his wife, feeling her warmth against him, hoping he'd drop off quickly too. He had a long day ahead in the morning.

It was a moonless night, and the room was pitch black. Alan, whose sleep had been delayed by thoughts of problems to be addressed when he got back to work, was shifting about in bed, seeking a comfortable position, when he stopped moving and lay still on his side and listened. He could hear the sound of, what? Mice? Rats? A pattering, scratching noise. He concentrated hard.

Something was moving about in their apartment, or just possibly above it. As he strained, he heard it at last, the distinct sound of footsteps treading softly across the floor of the vacant flat above. One foot hesitantly after the other. Someone who didn't want to be heard.

"What the hell was that?" he muttered under his breath. "The place is empty."

Turning on to his back, Alan stared up at the ceiling and breathed in deeply. At first there was nothing. Then, he heard it again, like the shuffling of someone quite old, accompanied by the tap, tap, tapping of a stick on the bare floorboards. As the sound moved slowly from one end of the flat to the other, Alan felt himself involuntarily begin to shiver. Their bedroom was cold. An icy breeze caressed his face as though the windows had been left open. Except that, Alan remembered, Henrietta had closed the windows before they'd retired. Alan's stomach churned and he could sense the hairs standing up on the backs of his hands and forearms.

"Nonsense," he breathed. "Absolute nonsense", and he sat up and rubbed his hands together briskly to warm them. But then he heard it again, and the sound was clearer now, more insistent. It was almost as though it were making a statement. TAP TAP, TAP TAP, TAP. A brief pause, before TAP TAP, TAP

TAP, TAP. Then just as suddenly as it had started, the noise stopped leaving a black echoing silence in its wake.

Henrietta's breathing had continued regular and undisturbed, she seemed to have heard nothing and Alan decided against waking her. Nonetheless, his pulse was racing and he tried to subdue it with slow deep breaths. Got to be mice, he told himself. Got to be. Or maybe rats. He'd tell the landlord in the morning. It was then that he nearly shouted out in shock as he inhaled the unmistakeable scent of musk in the room. The old lady was in the room with them. Alan waited for the feel of her hand on his face or shoulder. She was here. Mrs Rosenfeld, their neighbour. Here. Now. He could smell her. Fighting to subdue his panic, Alan lay back against the pillows and started counting the seconds until something happened. Seconds became minutes and minutes became hours.

Alan slept little that night and his work the next day suffered. Determining to put the incident out of his mind, Alan rationalised his foolishness and was able to forget what he'd heard that first night in those that followed. No such thing as ghosts. All his stupid imagination.

Ten days after Alan and Henrietta had taken up residence, four unkempt, unshaven young men moved into the empty apartment above them. They brought large open containers of belongings and sophisticated looking electrical equipment.

Alan, experiencing a moment of disquiet said vaguely, "You know, I've seen them before, I'm sure of it; but I can't think where." Henrietta merely shrugged at him as everything was dragged in to the house. "Can't say I know them, darling," she said.

Two nights on, Alan studied till 1.30 am, then wearily turned in. He was absolutely beat, his neck and shoulders aching with the stress of a long evening's study. He had another long day ahead of him tomorrow including a number of clients to see. With the one recent exception, he'd never had trouble sleeping, and within seconds he was drifting off into a peaceful slumber.

An hour later, the new tenants arrived home. There was the sound of a key scraping in a lock, and muffled sniggering from outside. Then four big men crashed through the front door, and thundered up the stairs like stampeding cattle. Alan frowned in his sleep but did not awaken, whilst Henrietta sat bolt upright in bed. There were goose pimples on her chest and back and she was palpitating. She felt frightened. She had never heard anything like it in her life. She pondered for a while, panting tremulously. She would have to interrupt her husband's sleep. Finally, as the noise subsided, she decided not to alert him.

Henrietta lay down and, snuggled against Alan's broad back. She pulled the covers about her shoulders and sighed contentedly. The place was all quiet again and as she slipped into sleep once more, she and Alan were battered into consciousness by the heavy, BOOM, BOOM, BOOM, BOOM, of a live rock band. The whole of their tiny apartment jumped in time with the music. Thump, thump, thump, thump. The crockery jolted on the drainer in the kitchenette in accompaniment to the clamour before sliding into the sink with a crash. Now they were both wide awake and sitting up.

Alan muttered angrily through clenched teeth, "What the hell!" Then, as if receiving a revelation. "Of course, I remember who they are now; they're a lunatic punk pop group - call themselves, God in Heaven, if you can believe it. They've had a minor hit record; think they own the world. I'll go up and tell them to cut down the flaming racket."

But Henrietta restrained him, she looked pale and tired, "No don't, Alan, please. There's four of them, and they looked so, so weird to me. They can't be normal to play their music that loud can they? Let's just tell the landlord tomorrow."

"Normal? I don't know," he replied ruefully, "Old Mrs Rosenfeld had to put up with us. Tell you the truth, I never realised how bad it could be. You see we never played our stuff at night, only ever in the day. Not that that makes it any better I suppose. If you ask me old Rosy's come back to haunt us."

"Don't be ridiculous Alan." Henrietta's voice was tremulous and she nervously primped her hair. She looked tired and unwell.

"Well, alright, maybe I'm going over the top a bit. But how am I ever going to qualify as a lawyer if I have to sleep through this lot every night." Alan's voice was rising and he was aware of his own growing alarm. After dad's business reverses Alan had sworn he'd stick to a `safe' professional career. Not for him the agonies of a commercial life. A profession like the law gave Alan the promise of freedom coupled with independence. It was for that reason he'd elected to pursue it, despite the necessary commitment to months of arduous evening work.

But to gain that cherished freedom Alan had first to pass his exams. If he failed his finals... Alan had a sudden sense of being bound in handcuffs. It was then that he realised he was experiencing a feeling that was for him quite unique. For the first time in his life he was aware of what it was to be weak and vulnerable. A bit like an elderly lady who couldn't cope with loud music. His neck and head felt damp, and with exams looming this was no time to be faced with the problem of sleepless nights or else renewed flat hunting.

Husband and wife held hands and stared bleakly into the darkness like two frightened rabbits as the thudding of music and juddering of the walls continued. Alan wanted to do the manly thing by reassuring Henrietta that everything would be all right. But he was frankly too alarmed to think of anything but the possible interruption, or even ruination of his career plans. Henrietta refused to allow Alan to go upstairs and remonstrate with the neighbours. And Alan, despite his height and weight realised he could not hope to take on four of them if things got ugly. On and on it went without respite. Hour after hour. The couple clasped each other tight until four in the morning when the uproar finally ceased leaving a void of sound shimmering in the air.

Their impassioned complaints to the landlord next day fell on deaf ears. He shrugged with indifference. No one else in the building had complained, nor even commented. The landlord saw no reason to risk losing four tenants as opposed to two, and anyway, the incident was probably a one off.

The incident was not a one off, and for the next six months the two were treated to the most horrific bombardment of sound. The noise was more than anything Alan had ever envisaged possible; far greater than his own modest record player had produced. It invaded them mentally and physically, as though it were wired directly into their heads, leaving them drained during the day and terrified at night. In the mornings, Alan's head would be singing with the echoes of the music. It was beyond all that was normal, all that was human. The police were unable to assist; the matter was private they said, and they had no jurisdiction.

Alan's studies were affected, of course, and in due course he failed his exams. He was horrified, had never failed an exam in his life. His father's dreaded predicament seemed to loom large. Failure screamed at him. The yearned for security of a profession tantalisingly beyond reach. A single exam was all it would take. It might as well have been Everest.

Henrietta's career was also stopped in its tracks and her health suffered. She became drawn and tired looking. Alan had noticed his wife was showing signs of premature greying. Freedom was now becoming an obsession with Alan. The flat was a prison, inhabiting it, a life sentence. No quiet, for him, meant no studying and no studying meant no escape. He was in a Catch 22 situation.

"It's her I tell you," he said to Henrietta one day. Alan had thought about it. He didn't believe in ghosts, did he? But then he wasn't sure what he believed in anymore. He was getting nervous rashes on his arms and legs. "I'm being serious, Hen. Mrs damned Rosenfeld's getting her own back on me through them." His hopes and dreams shrivelling, Alan was on the verge of tears. His life was falling apart, his plans for their future were withering on the vine. He felt something close to desperation. "We've got to move out of here before I go mad."

Henrietta searched the newspapers and agencies, eventually finding them a first floor maisonette, one of a purpose built block of four, in Theydon Bois, Essex. Alan's career was on hold, as he'd taken to driving a mini cab to earn the extra they needed to fund the enormous mortgage. His beautiful black hair now hung lank and greasy with stress, and he'd noticed, with consternation, how more and more of it was becoming detached from his scalp every day in the comb.

"At least we've left the big city behind," he said, trying to sound optimistic, as they hauled in packing cases of belongings. In fact he did feel better, the area was open and the air clean. Fields of cattle all around, and Epping Forest nearby improved Alan's spirits enormously. "Perhaps we'll get some peace now, and I can get back to the books. First thing though, an early night, and a decent sleep. God Hen! I just can't wait, I'm literally dead on my feet."

They both settled in to their delightful little home and at 10pm had just turned out the lights and pulled blankets up to chins when it started from the flat below. BOOM, BOOM, BOOM, BOOM. Alan jerked backwards as though he'd been kicked in the stomach by a mule. "I don't believe it; I just don't believe it," he bellowed. What is happening? Why won't the old bitch leave us alone? It's her, Hen! It's her I tell you! Old Rosy!" Then as though collecting himself, he growled, "I'm going downstairs to see what the hell this is all about."

Henrietta let Alan go this time, and he was back after ten minutes, smiling and looking relieved. He felt better. No problems with aggressive young thugs. This he could handle. "It's okay, it's okay," he sighed. "They're an elderly couple, hard of hearing. They like jazz and rock music, would you believe? They've promised to keep it down. A religious couple. Sweet really. Sign over their front door says, `ALL'S RIGHT WITH THE WORLD, whilst GOD IS IN HIS HEAVEN.'

Despite his demeanour, Alan was worried. Small wonder. The noise was following them wherever they went like a dog on a lead. And even if there were logical reasons for each incident, nothing explained the continued sequence of events that were driving them both to distraction. And, despite rationalising his suspicions as frustrated comments, nothing could account for the nagging feeling that the old lady really was laughing at him.

The elderly neighbours tried, but they kept odd hours. The brickwork was paper thin, and they kept on forgetting. A wall of sound would suddenly hit the Strongs at 2 and 3 in the morning dragging them from sleep and leaving them both exhausted the next day.

The other three apartments were just as bad; all retired couples who were deaf, or pretending to be, either playing radiograms or TVs on top volume; and always at different times.

Alan was becoming frantic, he was suffering dizzy spells and blinding headaches. "Old Rosy's organised it so they work in shifts," he muttered. It may sound crazy, but she's after us, I know it. I'm sorry, Hen, but I've given up the prospect of law. My head's bursting with this continuing nightmare. I'm going crazy. If it doesn't stop, I'm going to commit murder, I swear."

It was Henrietta who found the solution when she exclaimed one day, "God in heaven, Alan, how could I have been so stupid? And with my woman's intuition too."

Alan was nonplussed. "Sorry, Hen, you've lost me."

"She loved children Alan. Have you forgotten? Mrs. Rosenfeld loved children. We must have a child. I'm convinced of it. She'll leave us alone after that. I mean, if you really think it's her that's haunting us." She looked at Alan coyly and fluttered her eyelashes, giving him that odd little smile of hers. She was changing, Alan thought, uneasily, though he couldn't say precisely how.

They moved again, they had to; this time, to a tiny cottage in Sidmouth, Devon, close to the sea. They'd sold the place in Theydon in a hurry, and at a loss. This new home, which

Henrietta had located, was all they could afford. To Alan, a town person who liked to be in the centre of things, it seemed remote and cut off from the world, but at least the place was detached. No one could disturb their peace now.

Henrietta was just pregnant at the time. Her health, which had been a major cause of concern to Alan, appeared to have picked up, if only slightly, with fewer bouts of exhaustion and palpitations. Although, Alan was sad to notice, his wife's beautiful long hair was becoming ever greyer as their stressed lives took their toll of her health. Alan resumed his career with a local firm of solicitors, and the couple enjoyed a brief period of calm until a few days before the baby was born. Alan had reluctantly agreed to Henrietta's choice of name: Rosalynd, being his wife's middle name and her mother's first. He had to admit, he wasn't overjoyed at his wife's preference. She, however had dismissed Alan's misgivings as pure superstitious nonsense.

Realising he would need to get in as much study as possible before the birth, Alan had worked most nights until around 1am. He was suffused with a sense of urgency. If he could only keep up the studies until. Until what? He didn't know. But he felt that at last he might have a window of opportunity to finish off his exams at last.

This night he'd been at the books until 2 am. He rubbed the back of his neck where it had become stiff, and thought for a moment about Henrietta. She was going to be a mother, to his child. He would be a father. He smiled contentedly. The room had got cold without Alan noticing and it seemed now to be getting unaccountably colder. Alan shivered, hunched his shoulders against the chill and started putting things away, slipping sheaves of notes into folders and closing up books. His wife was right of course. There was no such thing as ghosts. It was all so much coincidence. All so much stupidness.

Then came the sound. At first he couldn't make it out. An indistinct scraping like a rat or a trapped bird trying to find a way out. A cool breeze caressed his cheeks like a kiss of silk and

Alan shuddered involuntarily. Then it came again. The sound. It was the soft tread of an elderly person shuffling across the floorboards directly above his head, together with a tap, tap, tapping of a walking stick. But there were no floorboards in the loft, only ancient rafters. Alan rubbed his temples and inhaled slowly. I'm not going to let it get to me again, he thought, as the familiar smell of musk lined the membranes of his nose. I will sleep tonight, no matter what.

Alan clenched his fists and gritted his teeth. But sleep eluded him.

She was a demanding tot, baby Rosalynd, and for months had them both up in the night while she screamed for hours on end. Every time they fell asleep, she would wake them. They were run ragged, and Alan was yet again forced to defer his exams. Henrietta looked weak and frail. Her face drawn, her hair now going white. Alan was appalled at the change in his wife, and in turn with his prematurely receding hairline looked older himself by the day.

Alan was somehow disillusioned, as if they'd lost out somewhere along the way. He felt at once guilty and at the same time angry. Mrs Rosenfeld. He'd done this to her, and now she was doing it to him. He was deflated and sad, his confidence waning. The world no longer beckoned and he only had himself to blame.

But he hadn't been this bad, had he? Of course not. Anyway, the hell with superstition. She couldn't beat him. It wasn't her ghost, or her malign influence. Such things simply did not exist. The old lady wasn't going to beat him. He ground his teeth determinedly No one could beat him.

Then one day, just after she had finished feeding Rosy, Henrietta had a fall. It was silly really, catching her toe on that bit of loose carpet on the stairs. It left her stunned for a moment. Alan had heard it and come running. She was all in a heap, feeding bottle and bibs on the floor, but not seriously hurt. "I'm alright, love," she'd said, blinking hard as she focused on her husband's concerned face.

It was then that Alan noticed something for the first time about his wife. Behind her long black lashes, Henrietta had one brown eye and one blue. Alan was kneeling, where he'd reached down to assist his wife, staring at her, stupidly. Ridiculous. How could he not have picked that up before? he wondered. The thought left him more profoundly depressed than ever before.

After the incident, the child unaccountably stopped yelling, and started cooing contentedly. Silence now permeated every corner of the home, wrapping itself around the family like a protective eiderdown.

"Told you darling," said his wife a couple of days later as Alan prepared some milk for their seven month old daughter. "I knew it, I knew it, I knew it. Mrs. Rosenfeld loved babies, she adored them. We've got it right at last. She'll leave us alone now, I promise you. Assuming it was her anyway," she smiled coyly.

Maybe Henrietta was right, Alan pondered. And a trace of the old optimism welled up in him as he thought about his law finals. Time to have another shot at them. "You're a clever girl," he replied kissing her on the cheek as he went up to feed the little one. Henrietta fluttered her eyelashes, girlishly, at her husband and self-consciously primped her now white hair, which for some unknown reason she'd taken to doing in an old fashioned bun.

A few moments later, Henrietta heard the sound of the bottle dropping on the landing, and frantic footsteps rattling down the stairs.

"What is it Alan?" She exclaimed seeing him white faced and shaking. "You look as if you've seen a ghost."

"I have!" he choked. "I have!" Alan stared back at his wife his pupils dilated to pin points, the whites of his eyes, bloodshot and yellowed. He knew now, knew beyond any shadow of a doubt. He was shivery cold through to the very fibres of his flesh. He grabbed her wrists, "She's here, Henrietta! She's right here in the bloody house with us." His voice, the quavering croak of an old man, hurt his throat to speak. "We'll never escape from her, Hen. Never! She'll be with us for ever."

"What are you talking about, Alan?" Henrietta's voice was trembling, her hands shaking and she seemed on the verge of tears.

"Come," he whispered. "Hear for yourself." And he took Henrietta by the hand and led her upstairs to the baby's room where he motioned her to say nothing. He crouched down on the floor outside the door and Henrietta followed his example.

"Gog gog gog," they heard from inside the nursery.

"Why, sweetheart," said Henrietta, happily, "that's only little Rosy talking to us. She's our baby. Heavens, Alan, let's not get paranoid."

Little Rosy? he thought. More like Old Rosy? I know who the hell Old Rosy is. But still he was insistent, muttering hoarsely, "Put your ear to the door and listen carefully. Don't say a word. Just listen."

And they eavesdropped together, ears pressed against the timber, their clammy palms clasped tight as the area was drenched in the sugary fragrance of musk.

"Gog gog gog," they heard.

Henrietta's face suddenly flushed pink and her lips went purple. She was panting and gasping, trying to catch her breath as though she were having a heart attack.

"Gogimma gogimma," the baby said, contentedly, trying to form it's babbling into more coherent sounds.

"Henrietta, what is it?" Alan begged his wife as she slipped awkwardly into a seated position on the floor, her back upright against the wall. "I'll call a doctor!"

"It's nothing darling, I'm fine. Absolutely fine. Just look after old Rosy for me, will you. I know you will." Henrietta smiled, that odd smile of hers, her eyelashes fluttering prettily. Then she was staring at the ceiling, her eyes, one brown, one blue, wide open and quite, quite still..

"Goggima, gogimma, gogimma," the little one gurgled on in delight.

"Goggima, gogimma.... gotimma....gotimma....gotimmal!!..

GOTT... IN.. HIMMEL!

GOTT... IN...HIMMEL!!!

Chapter Eight

DEATH ZONE, EVEREST.

"Daddy, daddy, daddy; please wake up! You must wake up! You must wake up!"

The little girl's voice filtered into his mind, octopus tentacles weaving their way into his brain. He was happy, comfortable, wanted to go back to sleep. So very comfy here. "Be back soon darling," he muttered. Back soon.

Then it was black again, for a time. How long? Couldn't say. Then, once more, only this time much fainter, far off; an echo in the mountains, "Daddy, daddy, daddy."

Strange dreams. Been having them a lot lately. He turned over in bed, snug; Teresa beside him. Darling Tess. Mother to Tiffany, five years old and more like her mother every day. Blond curls, turned up button nose, the cheekiest smile in Christendom. When she cooed, "Daddy please?" his heart melted, and whatever it was, she got her way. "You spoil her," said Tess. Then smiling, gave way herself to some trivial demand of the tot. How could they not?

The babe had been born with a congenital heart defect; the parents facing tragedy at the start of a tiny precious life. They called it an atrial septum defect. The septum separating the upper chambers of the heart, allowing blood to flow from the left atrium to the right, instead of down where it should have, to the left ventricle. The couple couldn't take it in at first. It had been spotted during a routine examination by their sharp eyed GP when she was two years old. A bluish tint to the lips and fingernails. "Probably nothing," she'd said. "But we'll have her looked at, just to be on the safe side."

Probably nothing? They'd caught it in time. But if she were to survive it would require surgery. "Chances are good; at the very least, fifty, fifty," the New York surgeon had said, kindly. But they knew he was only trying to bolster their morale. Still she was a fighter. My God! What a fighter. Fooled them all. Came through with flying colours.

"Dadeeeee!" Barely audible. Good girl, he thought and dreamed on.

His little soldier. Even at two years old she'd responded to Daddy's little pep talks. Picked up the advice eagerly. "Sweetheart, we're going to take a magic trip to a big city, a long way away. Daddy, Mummy and Tiffs."

"Will I stop being sleepy all the time, after the opennation daddy?" she'd yawned.

"You bet; but there's going to be a bit of an ache here and there. Going to have to be brave, Tiffs."

"Can Teddy have an opennation too?"

"Of course he can." And they'd put stitches in the furry toy's chest to match those on his little girl's chest.

She'd sailed through it, of course, the little one; giving pep talks to Teddy, like those Daddy had given her. "Now Teddy, I want a big smile from you. You're doing fine, just fine."

But Tess hadn't sailed through. The worry and the strain had nearly destroyed her. This was a very wanted child, Tess having had trouble conceiving; although not for want of trying. Tess loved sex, welcomed it joyously. Wanted it as much as James could give it to her. She was every man's dream. Easily aroused, coming quickly; then wanting more. Tow-haired, with an hourglass figure and disgracefully long legs, she'd been sought after by many men and had responded generously. There'd been literally dozens. "Well," she'd said, early in their relationship, before James had realised just how many, "I was never taught to be ashamed of sex."

"Daaadeeee!!!!" A faint whisper.

James had been intrigued. He'd married a tom cat. "So," he'd said one day, "all these relationships at the same time?"

"No," she'd laughed. "Hardly. Always one at a time." And always faithful to the one, until a relationship ended. Never be greedy is my philosophy, darling; there's enough there for everyone." She stood back, arms folded, the halo of curls framing her face.

James had raised an eyebrow at that last remark, but let it pass. If he admitted it to himself, he found the idea of his wife's multiple liaisons the tiniest bit erotic.

But her fears had worn them both down. James had a growing legal practice. International lawyers. High stress, long hours, high maintenance, high earnings. James had always liked a challenge. He was up for anything. Including the challenge of Tess, to which he'd risen admirably.

But this challenge was different. The practice was growing fast, going places, earning itself a name in the business; but it needed all James's attention, and all the cash he could loot from it in its early life to pay for the US surgery. Now, on top of everything else, he had to contend with Tess's fears, her nightmares, her inability to sleep. Up till now, Tess had been his rock, his mentor and inspiration. That is, if he ever needed one. For James was a self-enclosed individual. One who seldom needed that sort of support, though his wife's love, demonstrated that way, was wonderfully welcome.

But now, in a single moment it had felt as though the world was collapsing on his head. The hardest thing was to simply smile when all he really wanted to do was to turn in on himself, to cope in his own way. If he was the one to sort through everyone else's crises when they needed advice and moral support, he couldn't fail Tess now. Not when she needed his support so totally.

So he buckled under and got on with it. Buckled under? Odd choice of words, in his deepest thoughts. Tiffany's voice, a faint breath in the background. "Dadaaeee." Buckles, ropes, picks, tents. Crackers! Barmy! Old boy-scout memories. He stirred in his sleep. Heard Tess's voice now, as she reached for him. Been a long time since they'd had much in the way of physical contact.

Being newly arrived in the area, they'd got to know some of their nearest in the neighbourhood. Bloody neighbours right next door. Mousey little woman. Good natured really, friendly and helpful when they'd first moved in. But the husband, one of those arrogant hedge fund traders. Earnings in telephone numbers. Holland Park was ludicrously expensive. Far Eastern investors had put prices through the roof. James could just, only just, afford their house, with a mortgage that was through the ceiling.

Next door however, the Honourable Dickie Cazenove had paid cash, of course. Always snooping around too. Any excuse to come in to their house. "I suppose you're mortgaged, old boy?" to James loudly, one evening over drinks with a number of James and Tess's guests present. James surreptitiously clenched his fists, felt his hackles rise. "Probably paying tax too, eh? When you're earning enough you'll want to buy up one of those genius tax plans old boy. Probably more than you can afford right now, hey? Still, when you *are* earning enough of course." And the Honourable had gone on working his way through James's 15 year old malt.

After their guests had all gone that particular evening James had said, "He irritates me. Pompous little imbecile."

"Not so little," Tess giggled.

"What?" James frowned, as he helped clear away the detritus of the party. "What's that supposed to mean? He can't be more than 5 foot 8 at most."

"Not his height, silly." Tess stood with her hands on her hips, grinning hugely at her husband. She'd already changed into her peignoir, a magenta affair, slit to show the maximum length of a shapely thigh.

"Well what then? His bank balance I suppose."

"Honestly James. Do I need to educate you? Didn't you see the size of his hands and feet?"

"Christ Tess! What next?" James stood up from where he was wiping down a coffee table, absentmindedly folding a dishcloth.

"And the bulge in his trousers?"

"I don't know about the bulge in his trousers, but I do know I saw him looking you up and down all evening. Come to think of it, were you teasing him? His eyes nearly popped out when you leaned over to give him his drink. Décolletage doesn't even begin to describe what you were almost wearing this evening."

"Moi? Teasing? How could you James?"

"Easily," he sighed. "All too easily."

James had been brought up by an aunt, his father having absconded with the au pair when James was six, his mother having succumbed to cancer two years later. It had been an uphill journey, but James had won a scholarship to a public school in Worcester, where, as the poorest boy there, he'd learned to look after himself when facing the taunts of the wealthier pupils. By the time he left for university, at the age of eighteen, and 6 feet 4 inches tall, no-one was picking on him anymore. He was used to dealing with the empty-headed Cazenoves of this world; they were no more than flies buzzing around and best ignored.

There it was again, a child crying out for him. Far away. A tiny voice floating around his skull. He had to go to her. Had to go…….. But it was all too snug and cosy cuddled up to Tess. She smelled delicious, talcum powder and Chanel.

Tess had had a very different start in life. An only child, she was surrounded by aunts and uncles in what amounted to an extended family occupying a vast house in Wimbledon, together with her parents and grandparents. They always seemed to have guests staying overnight, and she became accustomed to seeing different people emerging from unpredicted bedrooms on mornings after. More than once, as a little girl, Tess had woken in the morning to find an uncle on one side of the bed, and an unknown guest on the other, while she, Tess, had fallen asleep under her quilt on the carpet.

James stirred again in his sleep. Couldn't seem to get comfortable any more. Now he felt chill, a shard of ice cold shimmied down his spine. Not snug now. Had to be up early in the morning; big case pending. He'd need to be alert, have his wits about him.

All he could think of was snow. Snow, snow and more snow. They'd said, whatever happens you mustn't fall asleep. Do that and you're dead. But James had always been a brilliant sleeper, could nod off anywhere. Wanted to sleep now. But couldn't seem to get the hang of it. Knew he wasn't supposed to sleep, but couldn't remember why.

Then there'd been the time when Tiffany had had a bad turn during dinner one evening. She'd suddenly looked ill, pale, pushed her food away. It turned out to be nothing, but Tess had momentarily panicked, starting from her seat to get to Tiffs, she'd inhaled a bit of the meat she was chewing. For just a moment James hadn't realised what was happening. Tess was going red, her hands on her throat as though she were trying to choke herself. Christ, thought James, she *is* choking. Dragging her from her seat, he turned her back to him and wrapped his arms around her middle, linking his hands together in a bunched fist, and heaved inwards, up against her diaphragm.

Tess coughed once and the meat dislodged from her throat, fell to the floor. They both sat down heavily. "God James, what was that?" Her voice was barely a croak, and she felt weak and exhausted at the realisation of what had so nearly happened.

"It's called the Heimlich manoeuvre," he replied casually. But Tess didn't know that it took all of James's self-control to prevent her from seeing he was shaking too.

"Where did you learn that?"

James touched the side of his nose, conspiratorially, "We hunter gatherers need to be prepared for all eventualities." Tess had seen the odd little gesture when she'd asked James, a couple of years earlier, how they were going to afford Tiff's operation in America. He'd touched the side of his nose in the same manner, and grinned, "We have ways."

He was colder now, icy hands gripping his arms and thighs, running up and down his chest and back. Just wanted to doze. The pillow, white against his cheek, was wet. How could it be wet? And freezing.

"James?"

"Yes Tess."

"You're getting podgy round the middle. Need a bit of exercise. Too many business lunches my love. All out of condition. I like my sexy men with a flat tum."

"You mean like friend Cazenove."

"Hmmm! Maybe. Come to think of it, you're right, he doesn't have a tum. A bit pigeon chested though."

"According to you, he doesn't need a chest, or anything else, with what you seem to think he has on offer."

Tess giggled, and put her arms around James's neck. Freezing, he shivered. "Now, now!" she remonstrated. "Let's not be jealous."

He heard it again, her voice, inside his head. "James." A bare breath of air, light as a feather dusting the inside of his head.

"James! Please James. You've got to move." Tess was stirring in her sleep. Reaching out for him.

His chest hurt, felt as though it was confined by a steel band, tightening at every moment. Couldn't breathe. He felt himself gasp, despite the oxygen supply; breath getting shorter, pulse slowing. Mustn't end up like Green Boots. What a prospect! Twenty six thousand feet. The death zone. If you started to linger or fail, they left you. Left you to die. Couldn't put the rest of the party at risk.

That's what'd happened to Green Boots, and over the years at least 200 others on the mountain. Green Boots, red jacket and blue trousers. Very picturesque. An experienced Indian climber, Tsewang Paljor, a member of the Tibetan Border Police, they said; with a party of eight in 1996, the year several had died in a multiple tragedy. With the weather closing in, several of Boots's party had turned back, but Boots and two others had gone on, foolishly. Boots had sought shelter in an outcrop on the mountain and, exhausted, unable to move on, had frozen to death. The other two had never been seen again.

Wasn't going to happen to him though. Three years of hard training; the most gruelling three years of his life, in order to attain what had become his life's obsession. The big one. Everest. Partly because James liked a challenge and this was as big a challenge as it got. Partly because he wanted to reconnect with himself after the traumas of Tiffany. Anyway, had to get rid of that tum.

Never climbed a mountain in his life, but this one was a cinch, they said. Got to be absolutely fit though. Dozens a day reaching the summit, just don't do anything silly, don't be a macho man. Keep it by the book.

And then, after all, be prepared to die. Everest can be unforgiving to the weak. So many stories to be told by the mountain. So many tales of courage followed by tragedy. Some years ago two men were climbing together; the younger of the pair, a man in his thirties, had started to flag. Struggled on for as long as he could. Finally came to a stop. Unable to move any further. The older one knew his companion was dying. Offered him the only sustenance he had left in his pack, some salted peanuts. Noticed that the younger one started to perk up. If he'd only capitalised on that, the younger man might have survived; but the older one simply remarked that dying was something personal and not to be intruded upon. The press had said the older man was a powerful personality, totally unafraid to die. And equally disinterested in saving his colleague. Sometimes, simply diverting attention from disaster to anything that captured the attention might be sufficient to salvage a life. But someone has to commit.

"Why're you doing it anyway?" they'd all asked James. "Because it is there." He'd responded, a trifle overconfidently?

"Daddeee," murmured now. Then Tess's authoritative voice. "Bed Tiffany; Daddy will be home soon.

Tess's voice again, pleading. Like one on their knees begging for mercy, "James; can you hear me? You got separated from your party. They couldn't move you. You're on a ledge overhanging a steep slope. You must try. Darling you must try. If you can just get over the edge you'll be able to slide down at least a hundred feet, out of the death zone. They'll be there waiting for you; the others.

He tried to open his eyes, to move on, but the effort was too great, fight leeching from his body. So very tired. Limbs not functioning. Freezing stiffness filtering through his muscles and bones. Blackness wrapping itself around him again. Poor old Green Boots. James's boots weren't green, they were brown. What was that old cockney song, Brahn Boots, sung by Stanley Holloway. Sleep, heavenly sleep.

Then he heard Tess in the next room, talking to that fool Cazenove. What the hell was Cazenove doing in the house at this time of night? He could hear the two of them murmuring together. Whispered entreaties. Not possible. He listened hard. "Darling, not now. James…!!"

She was talking to him, to James. Or if not him, to whom? Cazenove? Not bloody Cazenove. What the hell!!

"Yes, sweetie, now." James could hear Cazenove's voice clearly on his mobile. Christ, he wasn't home at all. He was on this bloody mountain, and he was dying. "You don't say yes to a gentleman and then change your mind, madam. Don't you know it's not ladylike." Cazenove's smug voice.

"Who said I was ladylike?" Tess wasn't protesting the jerk,

she was sounding coy. Not possible. What was she doing with the man?

"Ooooh! Dickie, you are a naughty boy. You're not supposed to touch there. That's only for James, when he's a good boy."

"And you're an extremely naughty girl. God! Look at those legs, they go on for ever. A natural blond too. James doesn't know what he's missing up there. Had to prove he was a macho man, didn't he."

James forced himself up on to his elbows, looked over the edge to the slope below, but fell back unable to move. He was alert now, fading fast, and he knew it. Anchored to the spot. Nailed down; crucified by ice. With that scum back home with his wife.

Then he heard Tess's voice again, clearly through the headphones, hoarse with desire. "Now Dickie, now, please. God; Christ, you're big. So fucking big."

"Nooooooo!!!" roared James. "Not with my wife you fucking bastard." He was up on his elbows again, strength flagging once more, leaden limbs. He inched closer to the lip of the ledge, knowing he'd never make it. Hopeless. His veins were filled with freezing mud, weighing him down. Snow was falling now, piling on and around him. He was becoming part of a giant snowdrift.

"God in heaven Dickie," she was gasping now, gasping. You're making me come and come again. Don't stop, please please don't stop."

Again, an effort, like trying to uproot a tree, making himself edge closer and closer.

Tess screamed, "Wooooow!"

James was bellowing, "No way! No way!" He was hanging over the edge. Still couldn't make that last bit. Oblivion closing in on him, finally.

"God, Dickie, you're beautiful. You're better than James. That's the best. The best fuck ever. Hmmmm!" She smiled, "Dickie's got a gorgeous dickie."

"Tess, you are a one off little madam. I always wondered what it'd be like screwing James's lady. Never thought I'd get to find out."

"Again, Dickie darling? Could you?"

"Could I? Thought you'd never ask."

"That mutherfucker's screwing my wife," James pulled, dragged, bullied limbs tearing in agony, joints, tendons, ancient bones, and began to slide, just a short distance, imperceptibly. Then he stopped. The vision of that creep and his wife beyond bearing. He moved his arms, now paddling frantically, was moving again, sliding faster now, and could hear distant voices through his fogged up head.

"Hey! Hey guys! Look, up there. It's James. He's made it over the lip. And he's coming this way." A great cheer went up from the team. "The man is actually going to make it. Boys, James is going to make it!"

James recovered quickly; he'd been very fit. That and his natural strength had seen him through. Just. But things had come close to disaster.

Over breakfast one morning, James took a sip from his scalding mug of coffee. "I had the weirdest dreams while I was up there you know."

"Really darling?" Tess was putting out Tiff's cereal, pouring milk over it. "They do say climbers can find themselves hallucinating in those dreadful conditions. Anyway, what did you dream?"

"You won't believe this, Tess, but I dreamed that you and our honourable next door neighbour were…….."

"Were what, James?"

"You know. You and he were…."

"HAH!!!" She practically shouted. "You have simply GOT to be joking."

"I thought you liked men with flat tums, that's what you said, and, well……big hands and feet, with whatever they come with." James, looking down at his steaming mug sounded uncharacteristically sheepish.

"Idiot, James. As if I could with anyone but you. And of all people, with that little worm." Tess shoved the cereal pack into the cupboard and helped herself to a mug, started to pour coffee into it, and sat down next to James. "Remember that story you told me about the two climbers and the effect of those peanuts? You also needed something to wake you up. She touched the side of her nose and smiled. "We have ways," she said. "I knew all about your odd little fantasies, even if they involved Mr C. So I gave you something to feed them on. It worked didn't it?"

"It worked," James sighed. "But my God, it seemed real enough. Tess, I swear I never knew you could be such an actress. I'd have said on oath I heard him talking to you. What a performance."

"The altitude," said Tess. "Fogs the brain. Anyway, why would I want a nondescript little man with a flat tum when I married a gorgeous big man with a six-pack? And what's more darling, you know I prefer my men to be circumcised."

Chapter Nine

ENDGAME

*T*wilight, and the man had been following them for a couple of hundred yards. She felt the hairs stand up on the back of her neck, a bead of sweat ran from her temple down the side of her cheek.

In black track suit and trainers he presented a spectral presence, practically shimmering in the encroaching dusk. But what really unsettled her was the man's white rubber face mask with its painted on mouth like Munch's Scream. From that moment she needed no convincing, this was no fancy dress get up.

The woman had crossed the road twice with her five children in tow and watched as he'd pursued them each time. He'd be approaching them at any moment now. Strangely, she was no longer perturbed. Under pressure she had the ability to be rational, to think quickly and clearly. Tall and well built, she reckoned she could defend herself if she needed to, and, in her experience, could talk her way out of almost any situation. Again, wearing flip flops and a summer shift, albeit split at the thigh, she couldn't have run even if she'd wanted to, and anyway she'd no intentions of panicking her children. She'd play things out by ear.

Although, with that menacing looking club hefted in his left hand, she realised that the man wasn't going to be amenable to discussion. But what did he want? And was she with her children facing an endgame?

In another moment, she turned around to find he was gone, leaving the woman puzzled and perplexed.

'SHE'S BEEN unfaithful to her husband you know. So often, it's practically become a way of life with her.' The elderly lady was what might be described as comfortably portly. With neatly coiffed white hair, sensible grey skirt and matching twinset, she was the epitome of middle class respectability. 'I suppose these days, anything goes. Like that old song. Except in those days, to quote, "a glimpse of stocking was looked on as something shocking;" today it's more like multiple partners being the order of the day. Even so,' she sighed, 'Saskia outdoes them all. She said herself she stopped counting when she reached the age of thirty. My dear, I said, what milestone had you reached? A hundred, she replied. I mean my dear, a hundred? And how many since? After all, she's thirty-five now. You know, she can't go on playing those sorts of games for ever. It will all catch up with her one day; mark my words.'

'You said she's very lovely,' the younger woman was kneeling down fastening her little boy's sandals. His freckled face had caught the midday sun and was slightly pink. 'Some Calamine on that nose, my boy,' she said to the lad, who smiled back agreeably.

'Stunning, I'd say.' And getting out of her chintzy armchair the other went over to a bookcase and took down an album of photographs. 'Just look, my dear. You won't believe what you see.'

Getting to her feet, the younger woman, tossing back her fair hair, straightened her knee-length flowered cotton dress and took hold of the album. 'Mmm,' she mused as she flipped through the pages, angling the book towards the incoming afternoon sun. 'I see what you mean. She *is* very tall isn't she, those legs, and that long black hair? My, she really is beautiful Vivien. You know, the white bikini absolutely shows off the tawny complexion. Magnificent is the word. A lioness. Wherever is she from? I can't place her at all.'

'Oh, it's all very exotic, June. She's from the same place as that singer Freddie Mercury, Stone Town in Tanzania. It's located on the western coast of Unguja, the principal island of the Zanzibar archipelago. Like Mercury, she's of Parsi descent, brought up in the Zoroastrian religion, which like Islam is monotheistic.

'Her father was a food market man,' Vivien went on, standing next to June and looking over her shoulder at the pictures. 'By that, I mean he had a tiny, plain concrete floor, lock-up shop in a suburb of the town selling all sorts of basic provisions. You know, big open sacks of grains and so on. Bottles and jars everywhere, or so she said. He struggled to provide for his family of wife, six strapping boys and Saskia. A self-educated man, he encouraged his family to better themselves and was overjoyed when Saskia obtained a scholarship to study law at Oxford where, unsurprisingly, she obtained a first class honours degree. God knows how she found the time between all the affairs. But, multi-talented, she later qualified as a chartered accountant too. *And*, she's fluent in several languages.'

'That is quite some lady,' said June, watching her little boy as he wandered over to the window to look out over the sea beyond the nearby cliffs. 'I'd have thought she'd find it pretty difficult to find a man to match those talents, yet she *is* married. To whom? I wonder.'

'His name is Mervyn and he's in that album you're holding. Actually, he's my nephew. Skinny little nonentity of a man, I'm afraid. Thinning mousey coloured hair, bandy legged. Am I making it clear?' June just smiled accommodatingly. Could he really be that disappointingly insignificant a person in the flesh she wondered? Vivien went on, 'She met him at university. I believe my brother pulled strings to get him into one of the lesser Oxford colleges where he read, of all things, media studies.' Vivien tried not to sound too disparaging.

'Oh dear, not the most inspiring of qualifications these days,' observed June. 'What does he do now?'

'Occasional editorial assistant at the local Islington rag. The odd article here and there. Circulation, uncertain. but minimal. The editor has big ideas; wants to expand readership. Mervyn seems to think he'll be called on to do more for the paper. Articles, and so on.'

Walking over to the antique drinks cabinet Vivien enquired, 'Wine my dear? It's not too early.'

'Please, Vivien. Anything red will do.'

'I've got a rather nice Malbec I opened yesterday.'

'Perfect,' replied June, continuing to leaf through the album. 'Now, is this him?'

'Jutting Adam's apple, pimpled cheeks, no chin, ostrich neck, vacant expression?'

'That's him,' giggled June, gazing back at Vivien. 'Whatever did she see in him?'

'Nothing very obvious, that's for sure.'

'Perhaps he's good, you know…'

Handing June a glass of wine Vivien offered, 'Where it counts? Somehow I doubt it. Have you seen the children yet?'

'I'm looking at a snap of five youngsters together. Three tall girls, utterly beautiful, like their mother, I presume. And two small boys, looking a bit like Mervyn?'

'That's them. My great nieces and nephews. Believe it or not the boys are older than the girls. But, as you've observed, small. Smaller in fact than their younger sisters.'

'That's a surprise. You'd hardly think they all had the same father.'

'And you'd be right. They don't.'

'What! Not the same fathers?' June sounded shocked.

'Exactly,' said Vivien. 'The two boys are Mervyn's, the girls were sired by three different men.'

'Good heavens! Well doesn't he know that? After all, it's staring him in the face.'

'Oh he knows all right,' said Vivien wandering over with her glass to stare out the window with June's son.

June cupped her wine glass in both palms, 'So doesn't he have something to say about it? I mean *three* different men?'

'All Mervyn says is, "I don't care what she does, or with who, as long as she stays with me."'

June took a long contemplative draught of the wine, enjoying the essence, 'Amazing.'

'It is isn't it. Still, I presume when love conquers all jealousy doesn't come into the equation. And Mervyn is very clearly not the jealous type. Just as well, I suppose,' she sighed. 'Crimes of passion are all very well in France. They wouldn't be tolerated here. Not that there's much passion with our Mervyn.'

'Still, you know they say,' put in June, 'that one in ten children is conceived with a partner from outside a couple's relationship. I never understood why, but I think I do now. Saskia wanted a better pedigree than Mervyn for her kids, and after seeing the first two results of Mervyn's efforts...'

'You're probably right my dear. I never thought about it quite like that. Does make it seem all a bit, you know,' she paused, 'Animal.' With that, Vivien sank gratefully into the armchair taking an elegant sip of her drink. 'She's due here you know, any time now. And there,' she said, 'I can hear her key in the lock.'

A moment later a tall woman swept in, with shoulder length black hair, skin-tight denim jeans and balloon sleeved white open necked blouse; it could only be one person. June felt herself momentarily breathless. Saskia's skin was flawless, her brown eyes enormous, nose small and slim, lips almost afro. She smelled of honey and cinnamon. She was quite simply, the most beautiful woman June had ever seen. When she spoke it was with a soft tone which carried the hint of laughter. 'High Auntie,' she addressed Vivien, whilst looking at June.

'Saskia my dear, this is an old friend down for the weekend with her little boy. June, let me introduce you to Saskia Behrana. Saskia's kept her maiden name, and just in case you were wondering, the forename is Dutch German in origin. Saskia's father was nothing if not far-sighted when it came to naming his daughter. His way of leaving people just a trifle confused. The two women shook hands and June said, 'Vivien was just showing me some of your family photos. Your children are very beautiful.'

'May I?' asked Saskia taking the album from June. 'The girls are,' she smiled, turning several pages. 'I'm afraid the boys look too much like "Soppy."'

'Soppy?' asked June, astonished. 'Who-ever is Soppy?'

'It's what Saskia calls her husband,' interjected Vivien.

'Well, he is a bit,' said Saskia, shaking her head as though to rid herself of something clinging to it. 'Soppy, I mean. I'm teaching him to cook at the moment, but he is a dreadfully slow learner.'

June must have looked nonplussed because Saskia offered, 'Oh don't worry. He's not entirely helpless. But he's a bit sort of vulnerable. He can write though, quite well in fact,' she added, echoing some of Vivien's earlier observations. 'But whether the paper he works on will give him much scope?' She shrugged, apparently resigned. 'You know, he needs looking after. Well, most men do don't they, but won't admit it. Mervyn knows his shortcomings and it's what makes him so attractive. I truly couldn't imagine life without him. He is my rock.'

Vulnerable? And, rock? Wasn't that a contradiction in terms? Resisting the temptation to raise her eyebrows in astonishment, or indeed to catch the aunt's eye, June said, 'Vivien tells me you're a lawyer? In practice, if I might ask?'

'Oh yes. I specialise in international law at Higson's in London. You may have heard of us. We're a fifty partner firm in that ghastly walkie-talkie building. Merve and I have a house in Islington, and I commute to the City. We come down to see Auntie for long weekends as often as possible.'

'And the children?'

'On their way. They were just behind me, but the girls stopped off to browse around the bookshop on the High Street, the boys to get ice creams.' Saskia paused for an instant, frowning as though worried they might have got lost. An odd flash of uncertainty. She'd had a momentary premonition, something, she couldn't say what, that left her uneasy. Chilled. Probably a recollection of the incident the other night.

June saw the change that had come over her, 'Are you alright Saskia, you look frightened.'

'I know it's silly,' she said, 'It's broad daylight, but I worry about them whenever they're out of sight for a moment. I'm a real old mother hen.'

Like a perfectly timed announcement the five youngsters breezed into Vivien's drawing room. The girls immediately arrested one's attention, being similarly tall and with the same hint of mystique as their mother. In denim cut-off shorts, white tee shirts and flip flops, their inherited bronze complexions, caps of curly dark hair and bouncing chat, their sparkle brought Vivien's place to life. All three crowded round a laughing Saskia, hugging her as though they'd been away for a year or more.

Vivien pointed them out in turn to June, 'That will be Namitah, the youngest, she's twelve. Nerinda is thirteen and Amrit is fifteen.'

'They're all so big and grown up,' breathed June.

'They all are these days,' said Vivien, then pointing to the lads added, 'The boys are George who's sixteen and Geoffrey, seventeen.

The lads, in khaki Bermuda's with short sleeve shirts and

sandals, had wandered in quietly, both finishing off their ice cream cones. Sitting themselves down unobtrusively in armchairs facing a TV screen they immediately turned to a sport channel. They hadn't ignored Vivien, they just didn't seem to be aware of her presence. Vivien glanced at June, the look saying it all without her having to speak a word. Even Saskia seemed barely aware of their presence.

'So tell me girls, what have you been up to? Let me see?' Saskia asked indicating the books the girls had bought, as the three of them circled their mother like a shoal of porpoises.

'Look mama,' said Namitah, the youngest and the most adventurous, holding up her paper carrier. 'I've bought Black Beauty.' Not a surprising choice given that she'd recently taken up riding for which she seemed to have a natural aptitude.

Saskia turned to her second oldest, 'And you, Nerinda, my romantic one?'

'I got Pride and Prejudice, mama. I can't wait to read all about the dashing Mr d'Arcy.' Nerinda had recently finished reading Wuthering Heights and had fallen head over heels in love with Heathcliff.

'Amrit?' her mother enquired.

'I got two books mama.'

'Yes?' Saskia prompted.

'I bought The Handmaid's Tale, and a book on self-defence, to go with my ju-jitsu class.'

There was something here to be expected in Amrit's choice, she being a physically strong and spirited young woman who'd take no nonsense from anyone. She'd often wondered at her mother's choice of husband, notwithstanding her love for her father. But, 'Self-defence?' asked her mother. 'You already go to a regular class. Why would you need to know any more about self-defence? You've never been attacked have you?'

'No mama. But that's not the point. I need to know I can take care of myself if I ever have to.' In what might have been an oblique reference to her father Amrit added, 'I never want to be reliant on any man to protect me.'

'So young and already so cynical,' Saskia intoned, thinking idly once more of the man in the Munch mask who'd left off following them as they approached Vivien's home the other day. Had she imagined the danger? Was it just someone in a fancy dress after all? Shrugging inwardly she buried the thought. At least the girls hadn't seen anything. They'd have been frightened and she'd have been hard put to explain away her own concerns.

Later, after June had gone she tucked up the girls in bed with a kiss and a cuddle. She was right, neither Namita nor Nerinda, who shared a room in Vivien's house, had noticed the man. It was different with Amrit, who had a room to herself. 'Night darling,' Saskia whispered, watching her eldest snuggle down, before finding herself faced with a question she couldn't answer.

'Who was the man with the white face mama?'

Pausing at the door Saskia debated how to respond; but realising her daughter wouldn't be fobbed off with any form of fiction, merely replied, 'I don't know darling. Go to sleep.'

'Do you think he could hurt us mama?'

'Why would he want to Amrit?'

'I don't know,' she admitted, sleepily. Then, abruptly sitting up in bed, she said fiercely, 'We're both big, mama. I'm almost as tall as you. We could handle it. I've done plenty of self-defence classes you know. No-one's ever going to hurt you. And we've got the boys, if they're with us.'

Dear girl, she thought, so flooded with love for her daughter her eyes pricked with tears. Ready to take on the world if need be. So much like her mother. Then Saskia envisioned her two sons trying to come to her aid in an emergency. Both as adorable as her husband and as about as effective. Or, more to the point, ineffective.'

'Sleep darling,' she said quietly. No-one's going to be

attacking us. Why would they want to? We've done nothing to hurt anybody. All just some silly prankster playing games,' she added, closing the door behind her.

Mervyn had arrived, almost unheard, when Saskia got downstairs again. He jumped up as soon as his wife entered the room, putting down the steaming cup of Horlicks Vivien had made him. 'Heh...Hello darling. Hello darling,' he stammered, his larynx bobbing up and down like a ping-pong ball. 'I got away to join you. Boss said I could leave early for the week...weekend.'

'Well now, who's my conquering hero? Thought you said he'd never let you go before 5.30pm?' Stooping down to take him up, Saskia threw her arms around her husband. 'I said you could do it.'

'You did. You said I could and I did. I di...did.'

Twirling with delight Saskia said, 'And he said yes, darling?'

'He said yes. That's right my love. He said yes. I could hardly believe it.' Mervyn was practically dancing around the room with pleasure. 'I never thought I could. But I can, and I did, I di...did.'

'Of course you did, silly boy. All you need is to have a bit of faith in yourself that's all.'

Flopping back into one of the armchairs, Mervyn picked up his cup of Horlicks, narrowly avoiding spilling it on his crumpled grey trousers, and sighed the sigh of the victorious as he sat back and crossed his legs revealing socks and sandals. Then, after a moment's thought, 'Lucimer's still out to get me though.'

Sakia frowned, 'Who's Lucimer darling?'

'Hmm? Oh, don't you remember, I told you about him a while back. Samuel, Sam, Lucimer from America. The boss's new blue-eyed boy. Wants my job, but doesn't write well enough to get promoted over me. Boss wants the paper to expand and was sounding encouraging where I was concerned. I was starting to make real progress, but now he's got Sam in his sights, and Sam's got me in his.'

'I wouldn't worry darling. This man Lucimer isn't going to shoot you, and even if the boss likes him, he's got to sell papers, and for that you need talented writers. That's you. I'm sure you're worrying about nothing.'

Mervyn looked doubtful, but put in, 'I suppose you're right.' Then he added, 'The man's a thug you know. He literally elbowed me out of the way of the copier today because he was in a hurry to get something done.' Mervyn shifted uncomfortably in his seat, then said pensively, 'Sasky, I'm not wrong you know. There is something about the man. A sort of hint of menace, if that doesn't sound too dramatic. Hard to describe, but when he gets annoyed you can smell his sweat from across the room, his voice goes from soft to a kind of rasp, as though he's swallowed a met...metal file.'

Changing the subject as Mervyn was becoming increasingly distressed, Saskia said, 'Drink your Horlicks darling and let's go to bed. You really are much too sensitive. If you did but know it, the man is probably more frightened of you and your talent than you are of him and his schoolboy bullying.'

Vivian sighed inwardly but said nothing, only wondering, as she surveyed Saskia, at the inexplicable choices some people make.

THE MAN ENTERED the hotel lobby, bare-foot and still wearing his wet-suit. He'd dried out in the walk from the beach and slung his flippers over his shoulder, but the surfboard under his arm still dripped water, earning him a reproving glance from the uniformed concierge which he studiously ignored. Once in his room he struggled out of the frogman's gear and engaged in his nightly routine of exercises, including fifty one-arm press-ups on each arm, five hundred sit-ups and fifty chinning's of the bar on a folding framework he carried in his valise. A hot shower, and his thick blond hair combed back, he massaged a variety of oils into the solid muscles of his arms, legs and torso before lying back on the double bed and contemplating his current engagement. With fees already agreed, a schedule would need to be determined. He'd had a sort of trial run. Got close to them, but not too close. Five of them with their mother. Been spotted, but not a problem. There was no hurry. Just a job, like any other, when the time was right. Most people died quite easily. Some cried, some begged, some offered money. Few asked why. Few fought back. They invariably knew.

On the rosewood drinks cabinet in the suite lay a white rubber balaclava with the terror stricken, wide eyed, open mouth of Edvard Munch's Scream applied. As innocuous as first it looked, it was yet as sinister as one of Dali's melting clocks. He'd be donning it again before long. Quite unnecessary really, it comprised his only nod to a bit of self-indulgent theatricality.

He worked alone. He lived alone, moving unobtrusively from city to city and hotel to hotel giving only the impression of being a surfer or scuba-diver on summer vacations. In winter he was a tourist, a walker. His false Swiss passport and credit card bore the legend, Albrecht Schlachter; loosely translated, A Slaughterer. His irresistible concession to vanity in metaphysical form. He banked in an offshore numbered account. For all practical purposes he didn't exist.

Helping himself to a whiskey from the drinks cabinet he paused for an unaccustomed moment of self-reflection. Alcohol helped him think clearly, taken in the right quantities. Life was a series of options, a game really. With the right choices the game could be prolonged and made more palatable, like his drink. With the wrong selections it all came to an end the sooner. Either way was of little consequence. His client was an individual with a clear mind and definite purpose, albeit with an outcome that would prove unpredictable. The motive didn't appear to be revenge, or money, nor yet jealousy. All so much more intriguing than any of the usual objectives, whatever it was his client, a hardnosed focused individual, had in mind.

SASKIA and the children were on their way back to Vivien's after a day at the fair. Mervyn had stayed in with a stomach upset. His usual nerves about almost everything. How could anyone want to go on the big dipper he asked. The very thought brought him out in a cold sweat.

Half term was over and they'd be driving back to London in the morning. Saskia would be at the wheel of the big Audi SUV. Mervyn had failed his test several times, and having finally passed, admitted he didn't like motorways.

They'd had a lovely day at the carnival, overindulging in ice cream, candy floss, pancakes, burgers and just about every other choice of junk food they could find. They all felt utterly self-satisfied.

Of course Saskia wouldn't risk leaving the children to make their own way back alone, particularly on these chilly nights with darkness encroaching earlier. And then, although the man with the mask hadn't reappeared, joke or no joke, Saskia wouldn't leave anything to chance. She was keeping the children close.

It was a beautiful clear evening, with the lightest of salt breezes to ruffle the hair. From the cliff-top path they walked, the sea, hundreds of feet below, reflected the moon in glittering pools and sequins of light, gently undulating with the swell. The comforting splash of waves could be heard faintly on the rocks below. The kids were dancing around their mother singing silly songs and laughing with recollections of their day and prizes won at this stall or that.

Amrit, having scored a perfect bull with an air rifle at the shooting range, had won for herself a wrist worn Vivosmart activity health and fitness tracker. The perfect prize as far as she was concerned. Namita and Nerinda had both claimed enormous teddy bears at the hoopla. The boys had tagged along somewhat disconsolately, avoiding the big wheel, the gondola swings and roundabouts, concentrating most of their energies on warning the girls of the risks of one ride or another, or otherwise generally complaining.

11.00pm. late for the youngsters, and the area was absolutely clear of cars, people and sound, save for the muted padding of their footsteps. They were ten minutes from home. Ten minutes from Aunt Vivien, daddy and hot bedtime drinks. A gorgeous day with lots of exciting things to remember and tell Auntie about. Amrit linked her arm through her mother's and they walked in step together, smiling and sighing happily in unison.

Then from behind them, the soft snap of a twig underfoot. Amrit saw it first and it made her pulse hammer in her chest. The black, skin-tight rubber suit shining in the moonlight, the hideous chalk-white mask leering at them. An almost snakelike grace of movement. Absurd. There might be nobody around to see, but why play such bloody ridiculous games. Why make yourself evident so that you might be, if not identified, at least spotted? Whatever the hell he was up to, they could handle it; Amrit and her mother, of that she was certain.

'Have you seen him mama?' Amrit hissed.

'I've seen darling. It's him again. Just keep walking and do nothing.' Saskia could feel the tension in her daughter's arm as it squeezed against her own. The other children ambled on, chatting among themselves, apparently unaware of what seemed about to unfold.

The man had worked out the timings well, mother and five children were on the cliff path that ran closest to the cliff edge. A long drop beckoned. Amrit tensed further, like a cat waiting to strike. Of course there was wooden fencing, but it was barely a metre high and they were practically standing next to it. One push would be all it would take. It didn't bear thinking about. But anyway, she repeated to herself, it wasn't going to happen.

'He's coming closer mama. Lookout,' screamed Amrit as the man grabbed Namitah by the arm. There was a flurry of confused movement of arms, of legs and fumbled activity before to Saskia's astonishment she heard her daughter growl, ' Kick him in the balls mama, I'll go for his eyes. We can handle this. I know it. We're bigger than him, she shouted, raking at the mask with her fingernails.'

But the man spun away from the two women, keeping hold of a terrified Namitah who stared, silently transfixed by the white disguise. 'Don't do anything stupid lady, or it'll all become more difficult. The voice was soft, educated, a slight accent? But yet unrecognisable. 'Listen to me and listen carefully. You're going to have to make a choice. Do you understand? It'll be the boys or the girls, or else all of them go. Over the top. Long way down. Up to you.'

Saskia's face was immediately drenched in tears, physically tall and strong, yet quite unable to protect her children, even with Amrit's help. The man still had Namitah by the arm and was standing perilously close to the cliff-edge. 'Why are you doing this,' Saskia begged. 'What have we ever done to you?'

'I don't have time for this lady. Make up your mind, and make it up now, or I'll decide for you.' He was getting annoyed, impatient, his voice losing its soft edge and becoming more of a rasp.

And then it occurred to her, like curtains opening, 'I know you, I know who you are? That voice.'

'Oh really? And who am I then?' The voice now become muffled through the mask.

'You're Lucimer. You're Sam Lucimer. You've been plaguing my husband at work. If you think this is some sort of joke...'

'Lady, this is no joke. Believe me. As for Lucimer, whoever that is...' He waited a beat, then, 'Time's up. What's it to be?'

Trying not to succumb to panic, and forcing herself to think with whatever time there was left, she visualised Mervyn, her lovely, but ineffectual husband and her equally feeble boys.

Would they ever amount to anything, the lads, so like their father, however much she loved them. Both now crying, clinging to her helplessly. At least if Mervyn were here, she reasoned. The presence of a man, even one as timid as he, might carry some weight.

But then there were her girls, so very special, all spirited, bright, showing such promise. Amrit, her eldest, ready to take on anything and anyone. The other two, terrified, yet calmly quiet, expectant, waiting to see what awaited. Life for them wouldn't be a series of burdens. It'd be a challenge. A game to be played. In them she had real faith. 'How can I choose, they're all my babies,' she sobbed. 'My precious, precious girls.'

THE VOICE WAS IMPATIENT, enquiring, 'What happened?'

'The older one tried to get clever with her mother's help. Pretty gutsy the pair of them. Strong too, had some basic ideas of self-defence. The others just looked on, said nothing. The boys whined a lot. Miserable couple of sheep. Two of life's classic losers.'

'So, after all that who did she choose to keep, the boys or the girls?'

There was a smile in the response, 'Who do you think?'

'I haven't any idea. Will you stop this bloody crap and tell me what was the outcome?'

'I'm curious to know how you thought the game would play out.'

'Is that what it is to you? A game?'

A sigh of forbearance, 'Life's a game. Yes? That's it. Beginning and middle. Then it all ends.'

'I'll ask you again, who did she choose to keep, the boys or the girls?'

'Obvious isn't it?

'Not to me it isn't.'

Moments of silence stretched away. Thoughts, words unspoken.

'Okay, I'll tell you then.'

A sardonic rejoinder, 'I can't wait.'

But still he kept him on the hook; the knowledge hoarded jealously. Finally, as though the fact were a charitable donation dragged from an unwilling sponsor, he announced, 'She kept the boys.'

Another long silence, and the comment, 'Did she then? And the girls? Where are they?'

'Are you kidding me? They're all dead. The three of them. It's a five hundred foot fall. Mother made a heck of a fuss. Practically went apeshit. Still it was her choice.'

'Interesting. The woman's unpredictable. Still, she likes the needy and the vulnerable. That's why she chose the man she married. Are the boys safe then?'

'Absolutely, you were clear in your instructions. Whoever survives is to be left alone. They'll be free to go with their mother when the police have finished with them. You know, I don't usually ask, but this is different. I'd say unique in my experience. Tell me, if you wish to, is it the outcome that was wanted?'

'It's what was expected, but it was necessary to know, to be sure.'

'She might have chosen to keep the girls.'

'She might, but apparently she didn't.'

'Chancy.'

'I'd say that's a bit rich coming from you, isn't it? Was there anything else? This is becoming tedious.'

'Just one thing. Say, sorry to break a confidence, but it's just occurred to me, I know who you are don't I?' He sounded practically jubilant.

'Do you? Who am I then?'

Your name's Lucimer isn't it? Sam Lucimer. Funny, that's who she seemed to think I was, when it was you all the time.

Who the hell were you getting back at? You must have had some pretty mighty grudge.'

'I'm ringing off now. For the record, she'll be the one needing the support from here on. Anyway, your fee will be paid by bank transfer as you instructed. You di...did well.'

Chapter Ten

BEADS OF BLOOD

The crack of the whip exploded in her ear, as a blade of fire knifed across her back. The woman screamed as the whip detonated again and again until her back was a filigree of blood. Her long black hair hung lank, unkempt, mixed in with the mess across her white shoulders. She looked like a Nazi flag, with colours of red, white and black. Her arms were extended wide by chain tethers at her wrists, linked to a bar suspended from the ceiling in the home gym. Wearing a black bra and thong, she stood tall, with her ankles slightly spread, the backs of her legs and buttocks displaying scarring from recent punishment.

"Too much!" she cried, "Too much. I can't take any more." Her body was a dead weight, a sack of lead, the chains at her wrists biting deep. He had to stop this torture.

"Too much? Too much? What do you mean too much?" A cultured voice. "We've the whole evening ahead of us. We've barely started." The man was in his late thirties, tall as the woman, taller, with luxuriant brown hair which flopped over his forehead. His bare forearms were thick and powerful, and furred with a brown fuzz. He wore navy pin striped trousers and a tailored, white, open necked shirt. He might have just come from the office. He probably had, just come from the office. His jacket was thrown carelessly over the back of a chair nearby. "Annette, darling; you really have been misbehaving disgracefully. You contradicted me at the party last weekend. Made me look extremely foolish. I know perfectly well that, A Doll's House was written by Ibsen, not Chekov. A mere slip of the tongue. We really must be brought to book I feel. But with the right kind of discipline, my kind of discipline, I'm sure we can put all that right, can't we now."

"Yes," she whispered. "Yes."

"I can't hear you, Annette. Speak up, woman; speak up."

But the woman had collapsed into unconsciousness and hung limp by her wrists, her head slumped over her chest. From above, she'd have resembled Dali's painting of the crucifixion.

She woke several hours later, drenched in blood and sweat; too weary to move herself, in too much pain to turn over on the bed she'd been slung on to. The man was gone and the house was empty. An eight bedroom house, with tennis courts, paddock, pool and carriage drive, sporting a Ferrari and a Bentley, in the heart of stockbroker Surrey. The Maserati was absent with its owner, on an errand.

The woman edged her hand towards her mobile on the bedside table. Every move was like razor wire being dragged across her back. Finally securing the phone, she quickly dialled 999.

"Emergency. Which service?"

The woman paused for just a moment, then said softly, "Ambulance please."

The doctor, a short, slender young man of far Eastern appearance, raised an eyebrow. "Ms Shardacre, I believe. We seem to be seeing rather a lot of you these days."

Annette Shardacre lay on her front in one of the hospital cubicles. Her back was covered with ointments and bloodied dressings. She didn't respond to the comment.

"Ms Shardacre, don't you think this is a matter for the police?

This is happening with alarming regularity. How long before you get killed?"

"No! Please, no! I don't want the police involved." The doctor meant well, dear man, but this wasn't going to be the way.

"Very well," sighed the doctor. "Your choice."

Days later, on an overcast morning, she was discharged. She dressed gingerly in maroon slacks and a matching, loose cotton top, and waited for the man to collect her. It was 11.00am. He kept her hanging about for five hours before he turned up. 4.00pm, her back was sore again and she wanted to sleep, but wouldn't risk annoying him. He swept in, clean shaven, groomed and in a brown leather jacket and tailored blue jeans. He looked beautiful and Annette noticed some of the nurses looking at him, wistfully.

"Hello, darling," a deep rich baritone. "Ready to go home?"

"Yes, Steve," she said, getting slowly to her feet. "I'm ready."

"You're in flat shoes, Annette. You know I don't like flats." He sounded petulant, like a small boy denied a gift at his own party. He frowned and gritted his teeth, furious. Then he softened, gave the hint of a smile, "I've bought you a gift darling," he said. "I'll show it to you later."

Annette smiled up at him, happily; expectantly. "I can't wait," she breathed.

"WHAT ARE those marks on your neck?" The coach, decked out in a tight white tee shirt and track suit bottoms, was heavily muscled and in his mid-forties, with close cropped blond hair and a nose flattened from past years of boxing. The gym was suffused with the stink of sweat and the hum of a crowd of exercise machines being hard worked.

"What marks?" asked Annette.

"Come on Annette. Don't be ridiculous, that necklace of red bloody scabs."

"Oh that!"

"Yes, that. It's either bruising, scabs or whip marks you seem to come along with. What in God's name do you two get up to? With your strength and physique, you don't need it. You can more than handle it. Or him. Or frankly anyone." Ed Martin had been Annette's trainer for the past four years, and in that time he'd come to respect her dedication and hard work. Ed saw his job as providing the client with the physique or the level of fitness they wanted, and that he felt they were capable of achieving. He'd noted that no matter how hard he worked her Annette kept up with him, pushing herself to levels he'd not seen in any of his other clients.

She was lying back on a wooden bench, legs spread, feet, either side on the floor, the iron bar across her chest supporting weights amounting to 80 kg. Annette, similarly attired as her trainer, was running with sweat, the white tee shirt stained dark between her breasts, her black hair plastered back like a horse's mane. Her back was pretty much healed, although, leaning back on the bench reminded her of how recently she'd been forced to sleep on her front. She breathed in deeply, held it for a moment, then pushing up hard, the weight lifted off her chest, moving smoothly till her arms were straight.

The trainer nodded, looked pleased. "You realize you're pretty well Olympic standard?"

"If you say so," she sighed, sitting up.

"I do say so. Annette, when are you going to wise up? This guy of yours is bad news."

"No he's not. Actually, he loves me."

The trainer looked down at the floor and shook his head. "Well he's got a funny way of showing it."

"Ed, please," she said. "Not now."

"Your choice," said the trainer, echoing the doctor. "But I'm telling you he is dangerous. Abused women? You could get yourself killed. Believe me, one day..."

"THEY'RE FOR YOU," said Steve. "A sort of 'Welcome Home,' present."

The box was flat, square, covered in cream silk. "Can I open it?" Annette asked shyly.

"Of course, my dear, they're yours."

She lifted the lid, and saw arrayed before her a necklace of rough-cut rubies. Dull, crimson, sharp edged, rocks. "They're lovely," she said. "But…….."

"But what, m'dear? Any difficulty?"

"No, no, Steve. They're exquisite. Absolutely beautiful."

"Of course they are. And you shall try them on right now."

"Now?"

"Is there a problem?" He had the necklace in his hands, ready to clip it around Annette's neck.

"No. not at all."

"Right then. Turn around."

She had her back to him, and he placed the necklace carefully around her neck. Fastening it from behind, he pulled from the back, the stones making a shallow imprint in her neck.

"Careful Steve. Don't want to break the string, darling." She smiled nervously, but had butterflies in her stomach.

He was pulling it tighter. "That's okay. It won't happen. They're strung on fine cable. It can't break."

Then, without another word, he yanked it tight. Annette, gasped, then screamed with pain as the stones bit deep into her neck, drawing blood, which streaked in ribbons down her chest.

"ANNETTE, when are we going to get your piece on abused husbands? And what's happened to your neck?" The features editor was shirt-sleeved; a dumpy, little, round faced man, with receding grey hair and a permanently harassed expression.

"Soon, soon."

"Soon, soon won't do. You're days overdue as it is. Off sick all last week. We need it now. And the neck? It looks pretty gruesome. Vampires in your house, is it?"

"No Hugh, it's the damn cat. When I was asleep. I forgot to feed her the other evening." She sat back crossed her legs, tried to look casual. But the job was important to her. She couldn't afford to lose it. The article would get priority over everything right now.

"By the way, Annette; we got an odd phone call while you were away. A complaint really." Hugh stood before Annette's desk, glanced disinterestedly down at the crossed legs. "A man, wouldn't give his name. Said you'd been questioning him about victimised husbands. Didn't like your tone. Said you were being over intrusive. Bullying."

"Hugh, what did this man sound like?"

"Well spoken. Deep voice. Articulate. Couldn't say more than that."

He was going too far, Annette thought. Steve, calling her at work? Making trouble?

"Told us we needed to give the job to someone else," Hugh added. "Someone trying to get you sacked? You're supposed to be a champion for the abused husband, not an abuser yourself."

"Forget it Hugh. Some idiot I'd guess. You'll get your article; give me forty-eight hours."

HE WAS BEAUTIFUL, with the physique of an Olympian, piercing blue eyes, and a boyish, open smile. They'd met at a reception for City financial people, organised by the newspaper she worked for, on the 32nd floor of the Shard. It was a late evening, London's lights sparkling, luminous, full of promise. He was a partner in a firm of stockbrokers, with a stratospheric income.

She'd felt disarmed, vulnerable at the sight of him. Her previous beaux had failed to ignite much real enthusiasm.

There'd been the accountants, the lawyers, bankers, businessmen, the various journalists with whom she came into contact. All pale apologies for masculinity in her eyes. Physically weak, when compared with her powerful frame, sexually inept, or inadequate to meet her rapacious demands.

Then there was Steve, a man, a real man, who ticked every box. In spades. He'd borne her to his home that first evening. A simple come-on line had opened the conversation. She'd been chatting to a group of guests and had turned away to look for something or someone more interesting, when she saw him leaning casually against a pillar in the room.

He grinned at her, hugely, and she felt herself turn liquid.

"Hi you!" he said.

"Hi you," she responded.

"What say, we get out of here? Go somewhere else?"

She'd followed like a puppy on a lead. It was new. It was unique. It was disturbing. She always kept her men waiting, spun it out, dangled them on a string until she was ready to sleep with them. Then she'd often disappoint them in the last minute by refusing. With Steve there was no waiting. She couldn't wait. It had to be now; tonight; here; anywhere. She was screaming inside for him, she was weeping for him, down there. It was a desperation, made all the more because he knew it. The smell of new leather in the Bentley, the crunch of the gravel on his drive, the little cottage in the grounds occupied by his housekeeper and the home itself. Massive, tastefully furnished, organised like Steve, and immaculate. She was a Disney princess in the arms of her prince. Dreams didn't come any better.

She'd disgraced herself on the drive home, unable to contain herself she'd reached down to his crotch and massaged his ample erection. He'd given her that smile of his, but not succumbed. He was just so bloody cool.

She wanted to have him on the floor of his hallway, but he slowed her down. A conspiratorial smile, a finger to his pursed lips, and he led her up to the bedroom. She barely saw the patterns of cream and taupe, the array of cushions on the king size double bed. She was tearing at his clothes, and when he slowed her yet again she started tearing at her own.

Thinking back on it she should have been embarrassed? Ashamed? What was she thinking of? What was she doing? She'd stripped naked, expensive clothes cast aside like rags and thrown herself on the bed, wantonly flinging herself wide open for him.

"Come on! Come on!" she'd urged.

But he'd granted her that bloody patronising smirk of his, and taken his time undressing. Then he'd knelt between her widespread thighs and penetrated a little way before stopping and holding still as she'd thrust upwards towards him in desperation.

"Steve, do it! Do it!"

"Say, please."

"Fuck you!"

"Please?"

"All right; please. Please."

"Please what?"

"For God's sake. Please, please, fuck me. Fuck me hard. You fucking bastard."

And she'd gasped with the shock of him as he'd suddenly swept into her. All of him, in one swift movement. Fifty thousand volts. She was shattered by it, numbed by it, unconscious and conscious again.

All her feminist instincts evaporated. He was a man. She was a woman. It was how nature organised things. Wasn't it? It was just that up to now she'd never met the right one. She'd cook for him. She'd clean for him. She'd bear children for him.

She told him she loved him, she adored him, she couldn't live without him. But he never responded in kind. Just that, now enigmatic smile, that left her feeling lost and alone. No matter how often she asked, he'd never commit himself to a declaration of love. His indifference was a form of abuse which she tolerated because of the way she felt about him.

But the sex stayed unchanging. Time and again she'd humiliate herself. Yet she knew it would be the same the next time and the next.

The first time he hit her the shock left her speechless. They'd been together about a month. She stayed over at weekends, but hadn't moved in entirely.

It was over some triviality. She loved cooking, and had taken to preparing an evening meal for them both if they stayed in on a Saturday night. There'd been a little too much salt on the parboiled roast potatoes. So he punched her in the face, blacking one of her eyes. Of course she'd made excuses at work and at the gym. They'd been believed at first, but as the beatings became more frequent, and the signs more obvious, she'd simply refused to discuss what she described as, 'Her private life.' Her trainer, Ed, had given his opinion, and he wouldn't add to it. What worried him, as he saw it, was the real prospect of Annette being killed. She'd responded, saying she loved the man and that was an end to it.

Research into spousal abuse for that article she was working on had indicated to Annette that, despite her brief, and perhaps as expected, the abuser was rarely female, the males involved invariably apologising profusely after each act of violence. Frequently, the perpetrator would lapse into floods of tears, promising never to touch their partner again. One abuser, after years of violence against his wife, always followed by his begging her not to go, had resulted in the abuser committing suicide when his wife had finally left, unable to take any more.

With Steve the pattern was different. He never apologised. The abuse simply got more concentrated, until Annette found herself succumbing to whippings that invariably left her hospitalised. But she couldn't leave him. He didn't need to ask her to stay, because he knew she would. He was like a drug she was addicted to. Something destroying her, but something she couldn't give up.

And yet despite the beatings and the humiliation she looked well. Steve stopped hitting her in the face, and it seemed to everyone she knew that she looked wonderful. Flourishing. Was she in love? They wanted to know. Only Ed remained troubled, despite her protestations that Steve loved her. Ed could see what the others couldn't, because she wasn't totally covered in her gym things.

Steve didn't mention the beads again. The rubies were left carelessly on the dressing table she used. A continued reminder of his ascendancy over her.

She was completely under his spell, in his power, unable to resist him.

Then one day something changed. A week went by without Steve disciplining her in any way. Neither verbally nor physically. Annette felt disorientated. At the end of the week she asked Steve if everything was okay. He'd responded that all was fine. But Annette wasn't satisfied. Another woman? Boredom with her? There was a difference in the dynamics of the relationship which Annette couldn't fathom. But it left her restless and confused.

She talked to her trainer, Ed. She'd just finished a round of squats and bench presses that would have left the average male fighting for his life. "I love him Ed."

"So you said."

"Something's happened. I feel sort of angry. Ignored. Even betrayed."

"Why, because he hasn't beaten you in a while? Come off it Annette." Ed was stacking weights on both ends of a bar for Annette to attempt a deadlift. "Why not just talk to him? Ask him if everything's alright?"

"I have, and he says everything is fine. I'm just getting so angry."

"Better watch that temper of yours Annette. I've never seen anyone lose it the way you do. Frightening if you ask me. Still, as long as you can work it off with the weights."

She'd prepared the evening meal. It was his favourite, roast lamb smeared with red currant jelly, hand cut oven chips, and sweet and sour red cabbage. Except, she hadn't smeared the lamb with the jelly, the chips were under-done and the cabbage was just boiled without seasoning. Then she served it up and waited for the expected outburst. But Steve ate the food, merely commenting on its being delicious.

They were in the dimly lit kitchen seated opposite each other at the breakfast bar, a half-finished bottle of Merlot between them. "Steve," she said. "What's wrong?"

He held his hands up, "Nothing's wrong. What should be wrong?"

"You haven't commented on the meal. You've said nothing. We both know it's not the way you like it."

"It's fine; it's delicious."

"No it's not. It stinks. I made it just the way you don't like it. Why the hell aren't you complaining? What's happening here? Tell me." Annette's voice had risen, and her cheeks were pink with anger.

"Alright, Annette. If you must know; I simply can't go on playing these games anymore. I'm not going to beat you. I'm not going to bawl you out. Don't you understand? I just can't bear to hurt you. I never could. This discipline thing started out as a sort of crazy deviation and it's progressed beyond anything I envisaged. But it's gone on long enough and far enough." He picked up the glass of wine and drank from it. "I love you, Annette, and you know it. It's me that can't live without you."

Annette gazed at him. Tried to fathom the man. "I can't make you out," she said.

Steve, smiling, got off the bar stool and came around to

Annette's side of the breakfast bar and put his arm on her shoulder. "Darling…" He said.

But she shook him off. "No!" she shouted and ran from the room. Steve raced after her, but heard the front door slam and her car starting, the wheels spinning on the gravel as she left the drive.

She drove recklessly along the narrow road, her heart pounding in her head. He frightens me, she thought. What does he want from me? I feel helpless when I'm with him; the original alpha male.

Steve turned over in bed. It was dark, but he thought he'd heard something, someone moving around. "That you darling? You back?" but there was no response. The sound seemed to be coming from the home gym, so he padded downstairs in his slippers to investigate.

In the morning Steve's housekeeper, Mrs Pettifer, an elderly lady who'd looked after Steve for umpteen years, went into the gym for its weekly once over. She'd ignored some of the signs of distress she'd seen there in recent months. It upset her to see her employer so troubled. He was a lovely man, gentle and considerate with everyone. But since he'd been seeing this one, this woman, he'd changed, become moody and withdrawn. The woman, for her part, ignored Mrs Pettifer, acted as though she was invisible. Still, it wasn't for Mrs Pettifer to suggest who Mr Earnshaw should be seeing.

But there he was in the gym in his pyjama bottoms, staring at Mrs Pettifer as she came in. He appeared tired; his lips and face seemed worn and grey. He looked as though he'd been up all night, his eyes, bloodshot and bulging with exhaustion. Poor boy, she thought. Poor, poor boy.

It was the police who discovered the note; apparently written in red ink.

"I thought the fucker really loved me. I didn't pay him all that attention just for this. Then he says, 'I love you.' Bullshit! I wanted a man not a mouse. No one says I love you, and thinks they mean it; not to me, and then gets away with it."

The press report merely stated. "Steven Earnshaw, a City stockbroker, was found flayed alive today, a necklace of rough rubies hanging him by a chain from a steel rafter.

ABOUT THE AUTHOR

My inspirations have come from real people, events or situations that have presented themselves. Titles like, I am a Contract Killer, I am a Gigolo, Death Zone, License to Kill, are all based on my own lifetime experiences, questions asked, incidents occurring.

Let me be reassuring, thus-far, nobody has been murdered on my watch. But the notion gave rise to the impetus to write my first murder mystery, The Lyme Regis Murders. Could I make the jump after years of writing macabre short stories to a full length drama? That familiar beating in the gut, said, Yes, try it. Give it a go.

And so to that cosy coastal town where nothing untoward ever happens. Or perhaps it does. The author seeks to shatter notions, change people's perceptions, spoil long held views. That was my intention in entering into the world of crime thrillers. I've found that nice people are not always what they seem. The helpless can be transformed into the most dangerous, the most dangerous become the most harmless. It's all up to the writer and what they're hoping to achieve.

For me there have been 10 children's books, 4 books of short stories and so far, three novels, with a fourth in the mixer.

Whilst a short story might be written with a flurry of adrenalin in the space of a few hours, a book will need more than just a flash of creativity. It will need perseverance, discipline and dogged determination.

But then, isn't that what is required of every ambition?

facebook.com/happylondonpress
twitter.com/HappyLDNpress
instagram.com/happylondonpress

ALSO BY ANDREW SEGAL

The Aberration Series of short stories

Book 1. I'm a Gigolo

FUTURE PUBLICATIONS

Book 2. I'm a Contract Killer

Book 3. Minor Aberrations

Book 4. Promenade of Mirrors

THE CONSPIRACY SERIES

Book 1. The Hamilton Conspiracy

Book 2. The Lyme Regis Murders

Book 3. The Black Candle Killings

CPSIA information can be obtained
at www.ICGtesting.com
Printed in the USA
BVHW072301170122
626430BV00002B/205